DEFINING MOMENTS

BY

CHRISTOPHER MCGOLDRICK

Outcast Publishing

Florida, New York

First Trade Edition: March 2014

ISBN-13: 978-0-9916108-0-8
ISBN-10: 0-9916108-0-6

Library of Congress Control Number: 2014903801

Outcast Publishing
www.outcastpublishing.com

Cover photo by Dmitriy Shironosov
© Dmitriy Shironosov/Stockfresh

Acknowledgments

Writing this book is nothing short of a dream come true for me, but I must admit, this is not an accomplishment that I celebrate alone. There are so many people that I must express my immense gratitude to for their unwavering support with this book, and with my writing career as a whole.

First and foremost, I want to thank my amazing wife, Kim, and my children, for always believing in me. I know this journey is one that we traveled together. My family saw me through each and every step of this experience despite the time it took me away from them. If it were not for their unending love, support, and encouragement I know I would not be where I am in life today.

I want to thank my mother for being a constant source of encouragement and support throughout my life.

I would like to thank Kerri Amberger for always being willing to read anything and everything I write. She has been the best proofreader, beta reader, and all-around literary guinea pig anyone could ever hope for. No matter what I send her, whether a chapter or a full manuscript, she always reads it right away and I can always rely on honest feedback.

I would like to thank Ben Burgess Jr. for his constant encouragement and support. He made me see that I was the only thing stopping myself from making my dream of being published a reality. If it weren't for him this book would still just be a number on my bucket list.

Last, but certainly not least, I would like to thank Sharon Vogt, my high school creative writing teacher. If it were not for her I never would have discovered my love for the written word. She opened my eyes to the literary world and made me see that it was so much more than mere classroom assignments. She truly made a difference in my life, and for that I will always be grateful.

This book is dedicated to
Brennon, Keegan, Rylan, and Makenna.
Always embrace every moment of your lives. All your
experiences, the good and the bad, play a part in making you
who you are.

DEFINING MOMENTS

CHRISTOPHER MCGOLDRICK

One

Just great, this is exactly how I want to spend my summer. Living in that house, in that town, where nothing is going to be normal. What I wouldn't do to just go back to the Bronx. Why did this have to happen? Why did this have to happen to me?

James was sitting in South Station waiting for the bus to come in. He was heading to his family's house on Tennanah Lake, which used to only be a vacation home. He grew up in the Bronx and all he wanted to do was go home. His father owned a construction business in the city for years and because of the poor economy he wasn't getting any work. Between paying James' tuition and the salaries of all his employees it became too overwhelming and the business went under. After twenty-five years of hard work, trying to be a good role model for his children, he lost everything. Their house was foreclosed on, his work trucks had to be sold, and the only option was to move into the lake house that James' grandfather had left to his dad.

The bus pulled up to the terminal and James

dragged his feet across the floor as he reluctantly walked through the doors. He hated this. He hated where he was going. He just wished he could stay at school and avoid going to that house. James hadn't seen his family since they moved up there. Three hours upstate from where he considered home. He tried to enroll in some summer courses so he wouldn't have to leave Boston, but being a philosophy major there weren't any classes that would fit into his curriculum.

"TICKETS...PLEASE HAVE YOUR TICKETS OUT!" yelled the driver as the line of passengers walked onto the bus.

"Here we go" James mumbled under his breath. "This is going to be a great summer, starting with the glorious nine hour bus ride."

The bus rolled off and James' stomach began to turn. All he hoped was that the nine hours would feel even longer. He hoped he could go to sleep and wake up somewhere else. Anywhere else. When he was at the station, standing in front of the ticket window, he even considered blowing off the whole thing and buying a ticket to the Bronx instead. He was sure he could find a friend to stay with for a while. Back at the only place that ever felt like home. At least he would be back where he felt comfortable. But he knew that wasn't an option. He had to see his family. His brother had just sent him a text message about how excited he was to see him again. As much as he hated that town he couldn't let Ryan down. The kid is only fifteen and he looks up to James so much.

James' cell phone vibrated in his pocket. He took it out to see another text from Ryan.

hey bro, where r u? r u on ur way?

He hated the way his brother wrote text messages. Some of his friends did the same thing and it drove him crazy. *Spell out your words*, he thought to himself, *your phone has a full keyboard.*

Yeah, just got on the bus. I'll see you tonight.

Before he put the phone back in his pocket it vibrated again.

Can't wait...this summer is going to be the best! Remember u promised to teach me to drive!

James put his phone back in his pocket without writing back. *I can't believe he remembers that,* he thought. *How am I going to get out of this one? I learned to drive up there when I was fifteen, and he has looked forward to doing same ever since, but I don't want him on those roads. I don't even want to be on those roads.*

James closed his eyes and tried to forget about it, but now he had too much on his mind to distract himself from where he was going. The only option he could think of was to sleep through as much of the trip as possible.

* * *

He woke up almost two hours later.

"Are you alright son?" he heard from the seat next to him.

He looked over and there was a man there. He must have gotten on at one of the stops along the way. He was an older man, probably in his early sixties with grey hair and glasses. The man was made up of a thin build, but his stature appeared to be rather tall and solid for a man of his age, although it was hard to tell exactly while sitting in those little seats.

"Yeah, I'm fine. Why?"

"You are quite the restless sleeper, and you woke up with a bit of a jump. Sorry if I seemed rude, I just wanted to make sure you were okay."

"Yes, I am fine. Thank you. It's just a long trip, and I have a lot on my mind."

"I see. Sorry if I disturbed you. Where are you headed?"

"Small town. Roscoe. My family has a house there and I'm on summer vacation."

"It's nice to have family, you are very lucky."

"Yeah I guess." *What is this old man talking about?* James thought. *He doesn't know anything about me, or my family.*

"So, you're on vacation? Where do you go to school?"

More questions, really? "I just finished my sophomore year at Boston College."

"That's wonderful. That's a very good school," responded the old man.

"It's a very expensive school," James said. "But they have an excellent philosophy program, and the professors are second to none."

"Sounds like you are a young man that truly cares about his education."

"I guess," James said as he turned towards the window. *The truth is I just care about answers. Philosophy al-*

lows me to look at what most people would consider to be un-
answerable questions and apply logic to answer them. I need
answers, I need to understand.

The old man was quiet after that, and James just
continued to stare out the window. Another two hours
had gone by and the anxiety James had been feeling was
beginning to subside. As much as he hated the town, he
loved the views on the way there. Looking out at all the
fields. The trees. The mountains. This was scenery he
never got in the city. Not in Boston, and certainly not in
the Bronx.

When he was growing up and going upstate in the
summers he loved being in the country. He loved being
out in nature. Fishing, hiking, going boating out on the
lake with his family, those were some of his favorite
childhood memories. But those days were over. Just
thinking about all of it brought mixed emotions.

The experiences he had up there were great. No
matter what happened at home all year long, it was like
a fresh start every summer. He had a whole other life up
there. A whole other group of friends. He was able to
express a side of himself there that didn't exist when he
was home. It was like an entirely different culture upstate. A slower paced life, a less full day, and a completely different type of fun. Different types of experiences. His friends upstate were so different from his
friends back home and he loved that back then. In the
city everything happened so fast. Everything changed
so quickly, and everyone always tried to grow up too
fast. Upstate it all slowed down and he could enjoy life
one day at a time.

His friends up there were from all over the place.
There was Danny from Connecticut, Sarah and her

brother Tom from New Jersey, and Joe and his sister Erin from Virginia. Then there was the group of people that lived up there all year. They were the most real of them all. Everyone else had that little bit of home that they brought with them, that little bit that shaped who they were no matter how much they tried to shake it. The ones who lived there, they set the pace for the whole summer. Everyone else just tried to adapt to lifestyle up there, and at the time, no one ever wanted the summers to end.

Most of the group didn't come up anymore. Joe and Erin's parents sold the house because it was just too much to travel that far. Tom and Sarah stopped coming up with their family once they got out of high school. And Danny… Everyone just lost touch with him. People grow up and move on with their lives, but James, he was stuck going back to that place. All those memories, the good and the bad, just staring him in the face.

Two

The morning sun broke through the window waking up Ryan at an early hour. He felt the heat of the light on his face, forcing his eyes open. He tried to roll over and avoid the light, but when he realized what day it was there was no chance of going back to sleep. He was too excited. It was the day James came home. Ryan would never come right out and say it, but he had been planning this summer for months. He couldn't wait to see his brother.

I can't believe it has been this long, Ryan thought to himself. *I know he doesn't really like it here anymore, but when we lived in the city he came home all the time. Since we've been living up here it's like he uses any excuse to avoid us. Well, maybe not us, but he is definitely avoiding coming up here. I'm pretty sure he hates that we live here now.*

Ryan got himself ready for the day and headed downstairs where he found his father already drinking his morning coffee and reading the paper.

"Hey, Dad, you're up early."

"Yeah, there is a lot to be done. I'm going to finish

that dock today."

Jerry Collins was the type that always had to be busy doing something. His most recent project, with a little help from Ryan, was building a new floating dock in the lake. When he wasn't doing that, he was constantly doing something else around the house or picking up handy-man jobs from the neighbors. Ryan knew that his father could never be comfortable doing nothing. He knew he missed the business that he had worked so hard to build, but he was too proud, or maybe just too stubborn, to ever admit it.

"You want to give me a hand?" Jerry asked.

"No problem. But I have a lot I want to get done today, too, so I can't spend all day on it."

Jerry responded with a chuckle. "What is so important that you can't help your father?"

"What a typical parental response," Ryan said back with a laugh. "James gets here tonight. I have to finish getting the room ready."

"You have been working on that room for days, it's not ready yet?"

"We have never shared a room before. I need to get all my stuff out of his way so he can relax when he gets in."

"I'm sure it's fine. I don't really think he is going to care how clean the room is anyway. You know how he feels about coming up here."

"Yeah, but that's all going to change once he gets here."

"Don't get too ahead of yourself Ry. I don't think it will."

"Sure it will. You know how much he loves it up here. It will all come back once he's here. Once we start doing all the stuff we used to do together. It'll be just like it used to be."

"I don't know bud, I wouldn't set my hopes too high."

"You'll see!"

Ryan and his father finished up their breakfast and got their tools together. One of the benefits of building a floating dock was that most of the work could be done on the ground outside of the water. Ryan enjoyed working with his hands. He must have gotten that from his father. It gave him a sense of accomplishment, made him appreciate it all that much more when he was done with the job.

Jerry and Ryan were looking over the plans for the last time before they finished the job.

"When this is finished it's going to look great." Ryan said.

Jerry designed the dock himself. There is going to be a section about four feet wide leading from the shore to the larger, main part of the dock. There it's going to be big enough for two lounge chairs, and a small table between them. There is going to be space on both sides to dock a boat, even though they only have the one that used to belong to Jerry's father.

"We going to put the boat in the water when we're done?" Ryan asked.

"I don't know if we'll get around to it today, we'll see what time we finish up."

It might be an older boat, but at least we'll have something for the summer, Ryan thought. *James and I can hit the lake like we used to. That will get him back into the spirit of being up here. He loves being on the boat, and he loves this lake, I don't care what dad thinks about it. This is going to be a great summer. It's going to be just like it used to be when we came up here for the summers when we were younger.*

Ryan remembered how much fun he and James had during the past summers. Now, Ryan was a permanent resident of the lake, but he still wasn't having any trouble getting excited about the upcoming season. He did have his worries about his brother coming back, but he had faith that it was going to be for the best, and that James was going to have a great time. He just had to be open to it and remember all the things that he loved about the lake. Of course he wouldn't let on to his father that he had these reservations. Someone had to stay positive. His father used to be so upbeat and always had the most optimistic approach to life, unfortunately, after everything that had happened over the last two years, it was no wonder he had such a dispassionate approach to everything.

A few hours had passed and the main part of the dock was finished and floating in the water. It was tied to the shore and Ryan was finishing the walkway section. Jerry was attaching the floats to the bottom, and making sure he had the sections in the right order. Together Jerry and Ryan carried the two smaller sections down to the water. They double checked to make sure they were placing them in the water correctly and then they got into the water themselves. They untied the main section from the shore and attached it to the middle section of the walkway. Then they walked it out to where it would stay and attached the final piece that would be anchored to the land. They hooked the dock to the anchors that Jerry had cemented to the ground and the job was finished. The two of them walked across the dock, doing one final check that all the boards were screwed down tightly and the joints where the sections met were fastened securely. They stood on the new dock and quietly admired their work.

"Let's launch the boat," Ryan said, breaking the silence with a somewhat excited tone.

Jerry couldn't help but show a slight grin. "I thought you had to finish cleaning your room?" he said sarcastically.

I'm pretty sure James would rather see the boat ready to go, Ryan thought to himself. "Yeah, that's not a big deal."

The boat had been sitting in the driveway on the trailer. It had already been de-winterized and the only thing they were waiting on was to finish the dock. So they hooked the trailer up to the truck and headed out to the boat launch just a half-mile from the house. When they got to the launch they put the boat in the water, tied it to the dock and then Jerry pulled the truck out to a parking space. This was always Ryan's favorite part of the season, the first start of the boat. Jerry turned the key and with very little resistance the engine started almost immediately.

"What a beautiful sound," Jerry said. "Your grandfather loved this boat."

"It's too bad he's not here to see it still running."

"The way he took care of this thing, he knew it was going to long outlive him."

They drove the boat back to the house. Jerry planned to go back later and pick up the truck. The ride was smooth, like the boat had never been taken out of the water. As they approached the dock for the first time Ryan jumped out and tied down the lines. It looked like the dock was going to hold with no problem. Now they were ready for the season. Ryan only hoped James would feel the same way when he saw the boat in the water.

Three

The bus pulled up in front of the diner and James dragged himself off. He got his bag from the luggage compartment under the bus and started walking down the street. Everything was exactly the way he remembered it. He walked past the gas station and reached Main Street. There he was looking down the block he remembered so well. The grocery store was just a little bigger than the average bodega in the city. There was the general store, a couple country shops, and the bank. *The epitome of Small Town, USA,* he thought to himself.

As he walked past the pizza place on the corner of Main Street the aroma became overwhelming. He had been on that bus for hours with nothing to eat since the morning. He didn't know how hungry he was until that fragrance hit his nose. He walked inside. It seemed pretty busy for a small town. He ordered a couple slices and a soda, paid, and walked back out the door. As soon as he was outside he started eating the first slice like he hadn't eaten in days. Blindly turning the corner, not paying much attention to where he was going, he collided with a jogger and they both fell to the ground. Now his soda was all over the ground, and the slice he was eating was all over his face.

"What the hell!" he said sharply. He looked up and saw a girl with blond hair, sweat beaded on her face, shaking off the hit and taking out her earphones.

"I'm so sorry," she said with exhausted breath. "I was really in the zone there. I didn't even see you coming."

"Yeah, whatever! Just a perfect end to a perfect day!"

"I really am sorry. Are you okay?"

"I'm fine. Maybe you should pay more attention to where you're going."

James walked off, wiping the pizza sauce off his face with a napkin, cursing his situation. "If this is a sign of what the summer has in store for me I should just leave now," he said to no one as he walked down the street. While he was walking a car pulled up aside him and honked the horn.

"Hey Jimmy! What the hell are you doing here?" a voice yelled from an open window. James didn't have to look to know it was Billy. He and James were best friends every summer since they were kids. They never spoke much during the rest of the year, but every summer it was like they just picked up where they left off the year before. Billy lived in town, and his grandparents had a house on the lake. It had been in their family for generations. It was one of the biggest ones on their side of the lake, and the first one you saw as you drove up the main road.

"Hey Billy, how are you man?"

"Not bad, haven't seen you in a long time. Why didn't you tell me you were coming up?"

"I didn't tell anyone. I didn't really know for sure until this morning when I got on the bus."

"Well get in bro, I'll give you a ride." Billy looked at the pizza on the side of James' face that he missed with his initial wipes of the napkin. "Looks like you need to get cleaned up."

"Yeah, thanks man."

James got in the car and Billy pulled away from the curb. They started the drive up to the lake and began to catch up.

"What has it been? About two years, right? You still going to school in Boston?"

"Yeah, it has been a while. I'm still at BC. What are you doing these days?"

He responded with a smile. "You would never guess. You are looking at a newly appointed New York State Park Ranger!"

"What? Like a cop?"

"Not really. I have very little authority, and only in the state parks. It's a pretty good gig, but just a stepping stone for me."

"Hey that's cool, you always did love being outdoors."

"Dude I hang out in the woods all day, ride an ATV up and down the hiking trails, and make sure everyone is having a good time. I'm on the list for the Environmental Conservation Police, so I'm just doing this in the meantime."

"Good for you man."

James couldn't believe it. Billy was always getting into trouble when they were kids, come to think of it, he was usually the ringleader. Now he really had a plan. He knew what he wanted to do with his life and he was doing what had to be done to make it happen. It should inspire him, but it only made him feel more lost. Billy was only twenty years old, just one year older than he was, and seemed to have his life so put together.

James had been so distracted by the conversation, and seeing his old friend, that he wasn't really paying attention to the drive. When he looked up at the road to see where they were he recognized it immediately. As they approached the bend in the road James could feel his entire body tense up and he inadvertently clenched the handle of the passenger side door. It was like the feeling you get when you ride a roller coaster for the first time. That slight feeling of terror that overtakes you, even though you know the chances of anything happening are almost impossible. Once they came out of the turn and made it to the following straight away the feeling immediately subsided and James tried to act like nothing had happened. Although it felt longer, they were only in the turn for a matter of seconds and he hoped his friend hadn't seen his reaction. James looked over at Billy and it was obvious that he hadn't noticed anything. A feeling of relief washed over his body and he relaxed for the rest of the ride.

A few moments later they pulled up to the small red house on Lake Road that James' father and brother now called home.

"Thanks again for the ride," James said.

"No problem buddy. What are you doing tomorrow? We should get together when I get out of work."

"I don't know man. I have to get all settled in here."

"Listen, I work until three o'clock. I'll give you a call

after that."

"Alright, I'll talk to you tomorrow."

It was getting dark by the time he got to the house, and if his father didn't have those lights running up the side of the driveway he probably wouldn't have made it to the door without tripping over something. That was another thing he never experienced in the city. The pure darkness of the night sky. Looking up at the sky was like nothing you could ever imagine. He was always fascinated by the amount of stars up there. Looking up into that sky always gave him a feeling he couldn't really explain, but whatever it was, it always felt so real to him.

He didn't have a key so he had to ring the bell. The sound of the chime hadn't even stopped before he heard the stomping sound of his brother racing to the door. It flew open with a fierce swing and Ryan was there to greet him like they hadn't seen each other in ages.

"Hey bro, it's about time you got here." Ryan made a feeble attempt to seem like he wasn't very excited, but no matter how hard he tried, the expression on his face gave him away.

Jerry walked out of the kitchen with a cup of coffee in his hand and a half surprised look on his face.

"Hello James. Why didn't you call? I would have picked you up at the bus stop."

"It's no big deal. I managed."

"Did I hear a car outside?"

"I bumped into Billy in town. He gave me a ride."

"Oh that's good, how has he been?"

"Alright I guess."

"You know he's a park ranger now," interrupted Ryan. He was friends with Billy's younger brother Jeff, so it wasn't surprising that he knew that.

"Yeah he was just telling me about it. A little hard to see though."

"It's kind of funny. You should see him in his uniform."

James and Ryan started to laugh thinking about the sight of it. "I'm going to have to make it a point to see that," James said.

Jerry jumped back into the conversation. "Sounds like a pretty good job to me."

They both looked at their father. "Yeah, yeah," they said simultaneously and they continued to laugh. It wasn't so much that they were making fun of Billy, or even that they disagreed with their father. It was just the way Jerry had said it. He was only in his late forties, but sometimes he just sounded like such an old man to them.

"I wish you got here sooner. Dad and I just finished the new dock and got the boat in the water."

"That's alright Ry. I'm not really in the mood for it anyway. It has been a long day and I just want to crash."

"Yeah man, of course. Well you know where the room is. Sorry we have to share."

"It's cool. Just take it easy on the snoring," he said with a laugh.

"Dude, I don't snore," Ryan said defensively.

"If you say so," James said sarcastically. He knew Ryan didn't snore, but he loved messing with him. Ryan always got so worked up.

* * *

The next day James slept in. When he got up there was nobody else in the house. When he went to the kitchen for a cup of coffee he found a note on the table.

Jim,

*I promised Mrs. Zurinski from down the street
I would help her with a leak in her roof. I'll
probably be gone most of the day. If you need
me I'll have my cell. You know where everything is.*

Be careful,
Dad

James held the note and stared at it both a little confused and a little upset. "So not only do I have to be here
all summer, but I have to spend the days alone?"

Ryan still had three weeks left of school so until
then he figured he was on his own. He just lounged
around the house most of the day not doing much of anything. When he really thought about it, it was nice. To
be able to sit back and not really have to worry about
anything. Now that school was over, and he didn't have
any kind of job, the day was his. He took a walk out to
that dock Ryan was talking about and couldn't deny
how nice it was. "They must have worked real hard on
this," he said to himself. The boat was tied to it and he
climbed in. He sat at the helm and reminisced about all
the good times he had on that boat. All the summers he
spent out on the lake. He could remember catching the
first fish he ever caught on that boat. He remembered all
the failed attempts to get up on the water skies before
he finally got it right. He laughed at the memory of himself crashing repeatedly into the water. He climbed out
and walked up to the house to get a lounge chair. He

dragged it out to the dock, set it up by the edge and just stared out into the crystal water of the lake. At that moment he felt more relaxed, more in tune with himself then he had in years.

He woke up to the startling feeling of the cold water being splashed into his face. He jumped up from the lounge chair and quickly looked around trying to figure out what was going on.

"Come on, get up you lazy bum," he heard.

"What the...Billy? What are you doing here?"

"Let's go man."

"You said you were going to call."

"Yeah, but I kinda got the feeling you were going to blow me off if I gave you the chance. So, here I am. Try to blow me off now," he said with a laugh. "Come on, let's go."

Four

He could tell James wasn't really in the mood to do much of anything. He wasn't sure exactly what it was, but he got a weird vibe from him the day before. He figured the only way to get James to come along was to keep his plans simple so that's what he did. When they got to his grandparents' house they walked along the path that went down to the dock. His boat was there. It was newer than the one James' father had and it was fully stocked with any type of fishing gear you could think of. Billy was a very passionate fisherman and always liked to be prepared. They climbed onto the boat and he did his routine check to make sure he had all the gear he could possibly need for the current exhibition. Once he was satisfied with his inventory of the equipment he untied the boat and pulled away.

After a slow twenty minute ride north he stopped the boat and anchored near the opposite side of the lake.

"This isn't your normal fishing spot," James said.

"Well it's been a long time since you and I fished together. This has been my starting spot for over a year now."

"Is it really that much better than the old cove?"

"Yeah it is. It doesn't matter what time of day I come here, there are always some bass just waiting for me."

They prepped their lines and casted into the water. They sat quietly as they waited for bites. The fish finder showed the spot was well populated but they had been sitting for almost twenty minutes without so much as a nibble.

Billy looked over and finally broke the silence. "So it really is good to see you again bro. I'm glad you came back?"

Without looking up from the water James responded in a serious tone. "Trust me, if I had anyplace else to go I'd be there."

Billy was slightly taken back by the unexpected comment. "I don't get it man. What is your problem these days? We always had such a good time here when we were kids."

"Yeah, well that was a long time ago. Things change. People change."

"Yeah people change, but they don't just vanish. I know you're in school and all, but you haven't been up here in..." He paused to think for a second, unable to put a timeframe on the last time he saw his friend. "I don't even know how long."

"Next month it will be two years."

"Two years," he snapped back. Then, just as rapidly as he started, he cut off his words and became silent. Instantly he wished he could take back his words as he realized why James hadn't been coming up. He couldn't believe he hadn't seen it before. He felt so stupid for not realizing. "The accident," he said remorsefully.

"Yeah, the accident." James stared off into the water, intentionally hiding his face as he held back his emotion. "I just haven't been able to bring myself back up here since that, ya know?"

"I'm sorry, I should have realized. I should have known. Sorry about giving you such a hard time."

"Don't worry about it. Let's just fish bro."

After that there was an awkward silence for a long time. Neither of them knew what to say after what had just happened. As time uncomfortably crept by they both got some nibbles on their lines but were unable to hook anything.

Eventually, Billy reeled in his line and put his pole back into the rack at the rear of the boat. He looked up and down the lake, checked his fish finder, and then seized the opportunity to break the silence. "Reel it in," he said. "I think it's time we hit up another spot. There is a good one not too far from here."

James did as Billy said and then went to the front of the boat to pull up the anchor. Billy started the motor and continued further north on the lake. James was a little confused. They always fished on their end of the lake. His house, as well as Billy's grandparents', was on the south shore of the lake. Now they were more than half way up to the other end. About a half mile away from the northern shore of the lake Billy was pulled towards the side again, this time closer to the shore than before. He cut the motor off and walked to the front of the boat to drop the anchor.

"This is as good a spot as any. Let's see how we do here."

"We are pretty close to the shore. Are we really going to get anything here?" James asked.

"This is a good spot. They love the shade of the cliffs and the water is deep enough that you catch more than just sunnies."

James looked around. He didn't even realize they were anchored under the cliffs. He now saw the face of the rock. He followed the natural lines in the stone to the flat surface above. They were far enough out on the water that he could see the small clearing in the woods were they used to hang out. There was a small group of people sitting up there that looked to be about their age. "So people still hang out up there, huh?"

Billy looked up from his line in the water to see the people on the cliff. "Yeah, but it's mostly people from the north shore these days."

The north shore was the end of the lake that had their own homeowners association separate from the rest of the residents. They had their own private beach, a boat launch, and a clubhouse that looked more like a country club. They were their own little community of what most people would consider to be mini-mansions. Most of them started as vacation homes, the same as the rest of the lake, but now just as many of the families up there were fulltime residents. Billy was never the biggest fan of anyone from the north shore. Before he graduated there weren't many of them in the high school so he only had to tolerate their 'self-importance', as he put it, during the summer. Now, by them living at the lake all year, more and more of them were in town and to Billy it was like they were rubbing their money in his face with their big houses and flashy cars.

While James was looking up at the group on the

cliff his attention was uncontrollably drawn to one person in particular. It was the sweat covered blond from the day before. He couldn't seem to take his eyes off her. There was something about her. Something he hadn't noticed the first time he saw her. She was beautiful.

"Who is that?" he asked.

Billy looked up at the cliff. "That's Mackenzie Green. The center of the world for the north shore guys. Why?"

"That's the girl that ran into me yesterday and covered me in pizza."

"Oh yeah? I bet she didn't even apologize."

She was standing near the edge of the cliff, laughing as she said something to her friends sitting behind her. She was wearing cut off shorts and a bikini top, a style not unusual around the lake. James watched, both confused and intrigued, as she walked closer to the edge ignoring the yells to stop he could now hear coming from her friends. She slowly wiggled out of her shorts and then, all of a sudden, she jumped. James felt his heart skip a beat as he watched her complete a full flip and then manipulated her body into a perfect dive.

"Holy crap!" James said as he jumped to his feet. "That was amazing. Did you see that?"

Billy looked over at his friend and laughed. "Yeah, I guess you could say she's a bit of an attention getter. Come on, if there were any fish here before they're definitely gone now." He once again pulled his line out of the water, raised the anchor, and pulled away in the direction they originally came from.

The whole time they were driving away James didn't take his eyes off Mackenzie. He watched her swim back to the shore and climb out of the water until they got so far away that she faded out of sight.

Five

It was their typical Sunday routine. They always started the day by meeting up in front of Mackenzie's house at six o'clock in the morning. Once Julie got there they loaded their bikes onto the back of the jeep and headed out for the trails.

Mountain biking was a long time hobby of Mackenzie's, but it was still fairly new to Julie. They were best friends, and ever since Mackenzie moved up to the lake they did everything together. Well, just about everything. Julie was never really into what she considered to be the 'crazy stuff'. Mackenzie always did the more extreme activities with her brother. They were always kind of adrenaline junkies. Julie didn't really get why a girl would be into those kinds of things, however, these days she felt she had to try to keep up with Mackenzie a little more. She was taking it slow, trying her best to learn the skills that took her friend years to hone. Jeremy had taught Mackenzie so much. They used to do it all. From the simple stuff like camping, hiking, and shooting; to the more extreme types of sports like dirt biking, downhill mountain biking, and kayaking through the rapids in the river. Julie used to think they were nuts, but now that Jeremy was gone Mackenzie has taken on the role of teacher, and Julie, that of the student.

The road stopped at the base of the mountain where there was a small clearing that served its purpose as a parking lot. To the right was a single path leading into the woods. They would ride uphill a bit until the path broke into a maze of trails spreading out into every direction. They tried to take a different one every time, but now that Julie was getting a little more confident, they always took the trails that lead up the mountain. At first this gave Julie the opportunity to become more fluent with the gears of her bike and learn how to properly use them. These days, it more gave Mackenzie the opportunity to instruct her friend in the basics of downhill mountain biking. Once they reached the top of the mountain they usually took the same two trails. The trails were very close to each other, and even crossed each other every now and then, but they were very different.

The one on the left was the one that Julie took. It was more designed for a novice rider to build up their skills and confidence. It was a narrow path with very sharp turns and even a couple small, introductory dirt jumps. The jumps were nothing too intimidating. To Julie it was always the speed, and knowing how to control it for each obstacle, that required the most attention. She was very conscious of the fact that someone with no experience could get very hurt on the trails if they didn't have the proper skills. The fact that she could ride it with such ease was an accomplishment for her, and she understood why Mackenzie loved the sport so much.

Mackenzie rode the trail to the right, and it was totally different than the one Julie took. It was designed for a more experienced rider. The turns were drastically sharper and utilized man-made berms, which were built out of the ground like curved walls allowing her to take the turns and maintain speed without braking. The jumps were built much higher, and most had gaps of about five or six feet. It was extreme and took a lot of skill to ride. She had seen people who weren't ready for a trail of that level get seriously hurt. They would lose control, unable to recover from a turn, and ride right off the berm. Some would miss the landing of a jump, or fall short and not clear the gap. She knew it was dangerous, but that was part of why she loved it so much. Another reason was that when she rode it she felt free. It was one of the most advanced trails in the area, and not a lot of people could ride it as well as she did. Jeremy always could. He could ride it better. Much better. She wished he were still there to ride with her. She missed him, and always thought about him when she was riding. She couldn't help it. The thoughts just lingered into her subconscious. She wondered if he would be riding with her if he were still there. If he would have made any changes to the trails to make them more difficult. The trails were already there when they moved into the area, but Jeremy did a lot of work on them to make them more fun. More...intense.

When they got to the bottom Mackenzie turned and looked at her friend with a very satisfied expression. "You're getting a lot better," she said.

"Yeah?" Julie responded. "How could you even tell? You were riding your own trail. Shouldn't you have been focusing on that?"

"Are you kidding me? I've been riding that trail for so long I could do it with my eyes closed," she said in her sarcastic tone. "Besides, you've never kept up with me the way you did today. I'm usually down here waiting for you. You *must* be getting better."

"I guess. I'm just really learning the trail. It helps to know what is coming up around the next turn."

"Talk it down all you want, but you're improving. You should be proud of yourself."

They sat on the rocks at the bottom of the mountain and drank some water. Mackenzie thought about when Jeremy used to compliment her riding when she was first learning. Him telling her how good she did always made her want to get back on the bike, no matter how tired she was. That was part of what made him such a good teacher, and why she was doing it now. She was always motivated to continue her hard work by the way he acknowledged her progress, and she incorporated that into the way she taught Julie.

After leaving the trails they got cleaned up and continued on with their usual routine. They went to the diner for breakfast and looked over the material they prepared for their class over the past week. This was a part of their day that they felt was most important. They helped run a tutoring class at the church in town for kids that were having trouble in school, or that had special needs when it came to learning. Mackenzie had a talent for working with children. She had a gift for reading people, and would always find a way to get through to them. She felt that if she had the ability to help someone, it was her responsibility to do so.

When they got to the church they were greeted with the most unexpected surprise. For the past month or so

Father Lipari had been at the doors of the church greeting the parishioners as they arrived. Father Lipari was a priest from the neighboring church in Livingston Manor, and he would fill in for Father O'Reilly when he was away on one of his missions. Father O'Reilly was the regular, and only, priest at the church in town. He also worked with an international ministry, and these days it seemed like he was traveling much more often than he used to. However, today when they pulled up in front of the church it was Father O'Reilly standing there, just as naturally as if he never left. He was greeting everyone with a smile and a handshake, happily accepting warm welcomes home.

Mackenzie got out of the car and wanted to run to him, but she didn't. She walked over and greeted him with a hug. "You're back! We weren't expecting to see you for another two weeks."

"Perhaps you prefer I leave again?" he responded jokingly.

"That's not what I'm saying Father, it is good to see you. How was your trip?"

"Same as always. Things are coming along very nicely over there, but it is always good to be home. How were things while I was gone?"

"They were good. Our classes are getting a little smaller now that the school year is coming to an end, but we have been thinking of other programs we could get started. Nothing ready to takeoff yet, but we've got a couple good ideas."

"Ah, it is nice to see you so passionate about something again."

"I'm just doing what I can, Father."

Six

James had been home for a few weeks and only left the house a handful of times. Jerry started to grow concerned, as any father would, and decided he had to find a way to get James out more. When he finally came up with an idea he knew James was going to hate it, but he had to do something. He knew Roscoe was the last place James wanted to be, but he couldn't watch his son just sit around and hide from the world anymore.

"Wake up! We're going to be late," he said while he tossed the item he was carrying on the bed.

James rubbed his eyes and responded with confusion. "What are you talking about?" He asked as he looked towards his father with half opened eyes. Jerry stood there looking down at him with his arms folded, obviously ready to start his day. James then tried to look at whatever it was that had just been dropped on his legs. He had to lift himself up onto his elbows to get a good look and he didn't like what he saw. It was a tool belt. Not just any tool belt, it was the one Jerry gave him when he was about fifteen years old. He hadn't seen that thing in years. In fact, until that very moment he had thought it was lost.

"What exactly am I supposed to do with that?" James asked, with a tone that indicated he did not really want to hear the answer.

"I have a big job, I could use your help," Jerry said. "Besides, you're not going to spend the whole summer in the house. You need to do something a little more constructive with your time."

"So I have to spend the whole summer schlepping lumber in the baking sun for you?"

"Hey, you used to like working with me. And I thought it would give us a chance to catch up a bit."

"Oh, is that how you're going to justify over working your first born for less than minimum wage?" It was clear he was now more awake and his sense of wit was returning to him. "Give me ten minutes, I'll be right down. But let it be known, this is being done in protest."

"Duly noted," his father responded with a nod. "Now get a move on, we're already behind schedule."

"Yeah, yeah. You and your schedules," James mumbled mockingly as he climbed out of bed.

Once James was ready they got into the truck and headed down the street.

"Hey, Mr. Schedule," James said sarcastically. "You know it's almost eight o'clock right?"

"Don't be smart," responded Jerry, "it's against your nature." He looked at James and continued with a jokingly sinister expression on his face. "And if we're late it's coming out of your pay...even if it is less than minimum wage."

Jerry always started work promptly at eight o'clock. He was a creature of habit and punctuality. The first and only time he ever broke that routine was right after he had to close down his company in the city. He didn't do anything for weeks after that. He just packed up the house and prepared to move, selling off everything he could in order to give his men an additional two weeks' pay to help keep them on their feet until they could find more work. He felt responsible for those men, and for their families.

They drove around the lake and headed towards the north shore neighborhood. About ten minutes later they pulled up to a large iron gate that looked like it should be protecting a fortress. It had been a long time since James had been to the north shore, but back then there was nothing this ostentatious. Jerry looked at his son and saw a confused and almost taken back look on his face.

"Who lives here, Bruce Wayne?" James asked with a disdainful chuckle.

"That is enough," Jerry said quickly. "We are here for work, not your opinion on security."

"Security…Really…I think this guy has gone a little overboard. It's no wonder Billy feels the way he does about these people."

"Enough. Not another word about it," Jerry said again as he reached out his window and pressed a button on the intercom.

"Can I help you?" a voice asked almost immediately.

"Yes, my name is Jerry Collins. I'm here to build a deck."

The intercom clicked silent and the gate opened. They drove up the driveway to the front of the house where they were greeted by a man who told them to pull

around back. Once they got to where they were supposed to be, Jerry parked next to a pile of lumber and
got out of the truck. James followed, verbalizing his desire again to be someplace else for the summer, and put
on the tool belt he hadn't worn in years.

* * *

By midday the deck was almost half done. They took a
break to eat a brief lunch and Jerry could see that James
was sore from all the hard work he was doing. Carrying
text books at school obviously didn't prepare him for a
summer of physical labor, but he was still proud of his
son. He knew his son didn't want to come here for the
summer, and he definitely wasn't expecting to work so
hard, but he didn't quit. They finished their sandwiches,
gulped down the rest of their sodas, and got ready to get
back to work. James continued to stack up a couple
planks of decking before climbing back onto the frame
to help his father screw them down into place.

The day had been relatively quiet, aside from the
occasional instructions Jerry had to give to his son. He
didn't want to come off as bossy, but at the same time
he didn't want to make it too obvious that he didn't really need his help on the job. What he had said when he
woke James up that morning was the truth. He simply
wanted to catch up with his son. No, it was more than
that. He wanted to reconnect with his son but it was a
lot more difficult than he thought it would be. He was
alone with James all day and he couldn't think of a single thing to talk about. He felt as if he was with a
stranger, but it was worse than that. To have this level
of awkwardness with his own son was...tragic. He
didn't know what else to call it. He loved his family, and

held that bond above anything else in the world, but with James it felt all but lost. He had originally hoped that this summer was going to reverse the direction that things were going between them, but since James had been home he hadn't seen any sign of that happening.

These last couple of years had been hard on their relationship. It had been hard on the whole family. They used to be close. Every summer James would work with his father's construction company, doing anything he could to feel like he was part of the crew. Every weekend the family would go up to the lake house and forget about their busy lives for a few days at a time. While they were there, although the kids had their own friends, the family got to spend some real quality time together.

Jerry taught his two sons everything he knew about being in nature. He called it his legacy knowledge. His father taught it to him, he taught it to his kids, and he hoped one day they would pass it down to theirs. They used to go hiking and fishing. Jerry taught them how to track animals and how to find their way in the woods. During the cool summer nights the family would sit together around a fire outside and talk about everything, and nothing, all at the same time. Those were some of the most cherished memories Jerry had of his family, but those days ended when his wife passed away.

It obviously wasn't easy on anyone, but James took the death of his mother very hard. He became detached from the rest of the family. He filed a last minute application to Boston College and left for a new city that he'd never been to. Jerry never told his son, but he understood his reaction. He was an adult when he lost his father and it hit him harder than he ever thought it would.

His father had been sick for a long time, and he considered his passing a blessing, but even when he knew it was coming he wasn't prepared for it. Then after losing his wife, his partner and best friend for nearly thirty years, he wished he could run away, too.

Seven

Working with his father wasn't as bad as he had thought it would to be. It took a couple of days, but he fell into a routine remembering all the things he had learned during those summers working with his father's crew. Skills that he thought he would never have to use again. But now, a week into it, his muscles weren't as sore anymore, the bruises on his hips from the tool belt were healing, and the sun burn he had gotten on the first day had faded into a light tan. Much to his surprise, the mornings weren't as hard on him as they were when he was at school. He wasn't sure if that was because of the summer air, being in the country, or the fact that after a full day of hard work he was exhausted and sleeping better than he had in a long time. He still didn't want to be in Roscoe for the summer, but at least having a full day kept his mind occupied. He didn't have time to think about why he hated it there so much, but he knew it wasn't going to be this busy for the whole summer. Here, despite all his experience, his father was nothing more than a simple handy-man. The people of the town gave him all the jobs they could for the sake of keeping the work local, but he didn't have a big company anymore. He didn't have a crew or any of the large equipment he used to. For those reasons there was only so much he was capable of doing.

As much as James had come to realize he appreciated keeping his mind busy, he found himself looking forward to the upcoming weekend. He hoped it would give him a chance to slow down a little and maybe spend some time with Ryan. It was his brothers last day of school and their father agreed to let him leave work early to pick him up. He hadn't told Ryan yet, but he finally decided to make good on his word and give him some driving lessons. James was still not very comfortable with the idea of Ryan driving on those roads, but he knew it was going to happen whether he accepted it or not. He figured a promise was a promise and he would be more confident in his brothers driving if he were part of the process. He never broke his word to his brother before and he wasn't about to let this be the first time. He planned to keep things simple at first. He knew Ryan would be happy with anything he offered, as long as it got him behind the wheel. Aside from the text message Ryan sent James while he was on the bus, he only mentioned driving lessons one other time. Based on the way James reacted when he brought it up, he knew not to ask again. James felt bad about that. He never meant to direct his displeasure of his summer towards his brother, but it happened more times than he would like to admit. Ryan didn't deserve that.

When the final bell indicating the start of summer vacation rang, James was sitting in front of the school in his father's spare pickup truck. It was just about as old as James was, with a fading paint job and a few rust spots, but the clutch and transmission were still in pretty good shape so his father kept it around as a backup. When he saw Ryan walk out the doors he pushed down on the horn, not expecting to hear such an unfamiliar sound. It was the proper tone of a horn, but you could hear the age in it, with an almost dying sound trailing off at the end. It was such an unusual sound that more people than expected turned to see the source. James felt like he should have been embarrassed, but he found it to be more amusing than anything else. Ryan walked over to the truck shaking his head and laughing. James could see that his brother was a little more discomforted by the attention gotten from the horn than he was, but he got over it quickly when he saw who was there to pick him up.

"What are you doing here?" Ryan asked as he pulled the door open and climbed into the truck.

"This is officially the start of your summer vacation. I wanted to help you kick it off properly."

"What does that mean?" He asked with a confused expression.

"You'll see," James responded, knowing his brother had no idea what he was talking about.

James drove off in the direction of the house, but about halfway there he turned off the main road. He drove down a bumpy dirt road, only a little wider than the truck itself, surrounded by woods on both sides. James ignored his brother's inquiries about where they were going and continued to drive without speaking a word. When they reached the end of the road it just seemed to stop, with nothing at the end of it. The woods that surrounded it cleared and in front of them was nothing more than some tall grass. James got out of the truck, walked around to the front and sat on the bumper. His brother followed behind him, still pretty confused about what they were doing out in a field.

"Hey, man," James said. "A long time ago, I told you I was going to teach you how to drive. I know I've been a little bit of a dick about it, but I don't mean to take things out on you. This is where Dad took me the summer before I got my permit and taught me how to drive. So…" James threw the keys in the air to his brother, "hop in!"

"Really? Awesome!" Ryan said excitedly. "I knew you weren't going to back out on me."

They climbed back into the truck, but this time Ryan climbed into the driver's seat. Being only five foot seven, when James and his father were easily pushing six feet, he had to slide the seat forward in order to reach the pedals. Ryan forgot that the truck was old and only equipped with a single bench seat so when he eagerly made the adjustment he ended up slamming James' knees into the dashboard.

"Ah, man!" James yelled out of both pain and surprise. "Watch what you're doing," he said while he readjusted the way he was sitting and rubbed his knees.

"Oh man, I'm sorry. I couldn't reach the pedals. Are you okay?"

"I'm fine. Just calm down and take it slow. Don't let this be an omen of how this entire experience is going to be for me."

"No, no…I'm good. Nothing like that will happen again. I promise."

Almost convinced James began to move forward

with the lesson. When their father taught him to drive they used the same truck that he and his brother were using now. It was the only one they owned that had a standard transmission. Their father was big about learning to drive with a stick. "Learn to drive a standard first," he always said. "If you can drive stick, you can drive anything, and you'll never be stranded." It was a good lesson, one that he appreciated, and now he was going to pass that knowledge on to Ryan.

"Okay, step down on the clutch and start the engine," he said.

Ryan did so with an excited grin and then looked to James for his next instruction.

"Now, put it into first and slowly lift your foot off the clutch."

The truck lurched forward making an awful sound and stalling out.

"Dude, I said slowly…"

"That was slow," his brother responded. "I don't know what happened."

"Listen to me, until you get used to the clutch you have to almost creep your foot up. Wait till you feel it catch and then give it a little gas. Just remember, there is no rush, take your time."

Ryan tried again with a much better result. He was able to get the truck moving pretty smoothly and even performed a couple figure eights in the middle of the field. After doing that, and learning how to come to a complete stop and then go again without stalling, they worked on shifting. The first couple of times shifting into second you could hear Ryan grind the gears a bit.

"Make sure you got that clutch down before you start shifting," James said.

After that Ryan got into gear fine but came off the clutch a little too fast again and James felt the truck jump into gear.

"Take it easy, you're doing just fine. Take it slow and just ease it into gear."

After about a half hour or so, it seemed like Ryan was getting it. Stop and go was no problem, he was working the clutch while maneuvering turns, and his shifting was becoming almost unnoticeable. James was surprised at how quickly he was picking it up, and he was glad that they finally did this together. This was the first James spent any real time with his brother since he got to Roscoe, and he knew it meant a lot to Ryan. He wouldn't admit it, but it meant something to him, too. It was the first real time he was able to overlook where he was and really enjoy himself.

As they finished their lesson for the day and were getting ready to leave the field James' cell phone rang. He dug it out of his pocket, looked at the screen and saw it was Billy.

"Let's see what this guy wants, huh," he said to his brother as he answered the phone. "Hey, what's up, Bill?"

"Hey, not much, bro. I just got out of work. What are the plans for later? Got any ideas?"

"How would I know of anything going on? You're the one that lives here."

"Hey, you've been here for what, like three weeks now?"

"So, just because I'm here doesn't mean I know what's going on."

Ryan interrupted his brother. "There's a party tonight if you guys want to go. The seniors do it every year to celebrate graduating. I was going to go with Jeff. It would be cool if you guys came, too."

Not being all that much of a party guy, James paused for a moment. Of course he went to parties at school, but this was different. Did he really want to hang out with all those people, most of whom he didn't know? Did he want to risk seeing some others that maybe he didn't want to see. When he thought about it though he realized he had been having a good time with his brother, and he might as well see if he could keep that going. After all, he was pretty sure Ryan mentioned it expecting him to make up some excuse for why he couldn't go and he wanted to see the expression on his face when he agreed.

He turned his head to his brother and responded, "a party, huh? Where at?"

"It's up at the cliffs. It's going to be an awesome time."

James turned his focus back to the conversation he was having on the phone. "Hey, you want to go to a party tonight?" he asked Billy.

"What, that senior party up at the cliffs? You know I can't stand those yuppies from the north shore."

"Come on dude, everyone's going to be there, not just the north shore crew. Besides, it's not like you ever needed an excuse to go to a party."

Unlike James, Billy was always into the party scene. As much as he tried to play it off like he didn't want to go because of his animosity for those from the north shore, it didn't take that much convincing for him to agree.

"Alright man. I'm on my way home now. I'm going to shower and eat then Jeff and I will meet you up there later."

"Sounds like a plan," James said, and then he hung up his phone.

* * *

There was no road up to the cliffs, only a path through the woods used mostly by hikers, ATVs, and off-road-ers. Those with four wheel drive brought their trucks up to the cliffs for the party. James and Ryan arrived around the same time as Billy and his brother and parked the pickup in a space near them. They folded down the tailgate and all had a seat on the back of the truck. Looking around it appeared everyone was broken up into their own little cliques. Most people were hang-ing out around the vehicle they arrived in, all of which were mostly pickup trucks and jeeps. They were all backed in in the shape of a semi-circle on the opposite side of the cliff itself. The rears of the vehicles were fac-ing the middle where there was a bonfire that could probably be seen by most of the homes on the lake. Off to the right, closer to where the north shore guys were hanging out, there was the keg sitting in the back of someone's brand new Ford.

Ryan and Jeff walked around talking to their friends and having a good time. Billy went to get a drink from the keg truck and James was left sitting in the back of his truck just looking around at all the little groups of people. When he looked over to find out what was tak-ing Billy so long something caught his eye at the car parked right passed the keg truck. There were two guys yelling at one another, getting closer to each other's faces, like they were both just waiting for the other to throw the first punch. James looked over at Billy, hoping he could just mind his own business. Billy loved to fight, and the fact that the argument was between a guy from the north shore and another guy from town, he wouldn't hesitate to jump in. James saw the look on Billy's face and knew what he was thinking. Thankfully when James looked back over at the crowd of boiling adrenaline, it looked like a girl had gotten between the two and calmed them down. As the group of spectators began to clear he was able to see who the heroine of the moment was.

"It's her!" he said out loud, despite the fact that he was alone. It was the jogger that knocked the pizza in his face. The diver that unknowingly captured his attention that day on the boat. It was Mackenzie. He couldn't believe she was there.

"What are you gawking at?" Billy asked as he got back to the truck with two cups in his hands.

"What? Nothing!" he said, slightly caught off guard.

"Come on, you were looking at something."

"The fight that was breaking out over there, you didn't see it?" he replied, trying to cover up his true interest.

"Yeah I saw it. I also saw it break up. So what were you still looking over there so intensely at? Something had to have caught your eye."

"No, really, it was nothing."

"If you say so," he said as he climbed back into the truck handing James one of the cups.

"Oh, no thanks, man. I'm not drinking tonight."

"What do you mean you're not drinking? It's a party, of course you're drinking."

"No, not tonight, Bill, I'm driving," he said, knowing it would get his friend to drop it, but the truth of it was he really just didn't like to drink. He had seen his friends at school, some really smart people, do some really stupid stuff while they were drunk. One of his roommates freshman year got so drunk he lit a bunch of his ex-girlfriends stuff on fire in the courtyard after a fight. Someone called the cops and he ended getting arrested and kicked out of the dorms. He didn't understand how people could drink to the point that they didn't act like themselves, but he knew it wasn't for him.

A little later into the night they were all still hanging out, just talking over the music that was coming from one of the trucks. James had seen some of the people he used to hang out with when he spent the summers there. Not people he really called friends, but they were friends of Billy's, so he hung out with them nonetheless. They mingled with some of the other cliques there but kept ending up back at James' truck. James kept trying to steal glances over at Mackenzie, hoping nobody would notice it. He couldn't believe how beautiful she was. Every time he looked over at her it felt like time slowed down. In that second it took him to look over he would play out in his head walking over there, introducing himself, wooing her, and them leaving the party together for someplace more private to get to know each other. He almost thought he saw her looking back at him once or twice, but he was sure it was his imagination. *Why would a girl like that be looking at me?* he thought to himself. At one point he got lost in the moment while he was admiring her and it drew some unwanted attention.

"So that's what you were looking at," Billy said.

"Wh...What are you talking about?" he responded, completely failing at his attempt to cover it up.

"Forget about it man, she's from the north shore. What would she possibly see in you?"

"Wow! Thanks for the confidence boost. Some friend you are."

"Hey, I'm sorry man. I don't mean it maliciously, but you know how all those people are. Especially the girls! They all think they are better than everyone else. Besides, she has been with Chad Wilson since just about the day she moved here."

"Chad? Really?"

"Yeah," Billy responded. "He's like the leader of the yuppies. They follow his every command like dogs. Pathetic!"

James knew Chad. Well, at least he remembered him. His family had been living at the lake just as long as James'. His father was one of the co-founders, and the acting president of the North Shore Homeowners Association. Because of that, Chad always walked around like he was the crowned prince of the lake. James couldn't think of a single person that could tolerate that guy. He didn't get what she could possible see in him. It was clear she could do better than a guy like that. He is nothing more than an over-pretentious, self-absorbed rich kid. Even if she is from the north shore, he could tell she wasn't like that. Just by looking at her it was obvious to him she wasn't like the rest of them. Besides, in all the times he had looked over at her during the party, he hadn't noticed anything that would indicate she was with Chad.

Just as James and Billy were finishing their conversation they heard someone yell. When they looked up in the direction of the sound they saw it caught the attention of just about everyone else as well.

"Come on," they heard Chad say while he was pulling on Mackenzie's wrist, "let's get out of here, this party is lame."

"Let go of me!" "Stop it! You're hurting me!" she yelled as she tried to pull away but obviously couldn't.

Instantly James jumped out of the back of his truck and was on his way over there. He didn't even think about it, almost as if it were instinctual.

"Dude stay out of it. It's none of your business," Billy said as he chased after him.

Without any hesitation James grabbed Chad, spun him around and threw a punch. He hit him in the cheek, knocking him back a step and causing him to shake his head in pain. Once he realized what had just happened Chad advanced back at him and James swung again, this time hitting him even harder and sending him to the ground. James was never a fighter and as he stood over Chad he still couldn't believe what he had just done. He felt someone grab him from behind and before he could react Billy was there tackling Derek Jacobs, Chads number one lackey. As they rolled around in the dirt James turned to Mackenzie.

"Are you okay?" he asked.

"What is wrong with you? What did you do that for?" she yelled.

"I thought he was hurting you. I was only trying to help."

"I didn't need your help. I can take care of myself," she snapped. Then she turned to her friend and said, "Come on Julie, let's go," and walked away.

Eight

Her blood was still boiling over what had just happened. *Who does he think he is?* She thought to herself. *Do I look like I need his help?* Then, before she could think another thought, Julie interrupted.

"How hot was that?!" she said with an obvious level of excitement to her voice.

Unprepared for such a comment Mackenzie turned to her with a look that clearly stated her disagreement.

"Oh come on, you're really going to tell me that you didn't find that in the least bit hot. Two guys, one of which you don't even know, fighting over you like that."

"Whatever. Guys are stupid, and they're even worse when they drink."

"It was more than that, Kenz. They were fighting over you. You should take it as a compliment. And another point I would like to point out, that guy that jumped in was really cute.

"Seriously? Is that all you think about?"

"Easy for you to say, I would kill for half the attention you get."

She hated when Julie made absurdly jealous comments like that. Not only did she get the same amount of attention, she was always more willing to accept it. Although neither of them ever had to struggle with obtaining popularity, it was always more important to Julie. She wasn't going to let her comment go unchallenged.

"Stop right there, Jules. You get just as much attention as I do, and I don't even want it. Please, you can help yourself to both of them." She paused for a brief moment and then continued with an obvious tone of sarcasm. "I don't need strangers swooping in like my own personal white knight trying to rescue me. I'm not some damsel in distress."

"That's just the way he is," Julie said. "Well, as far as I remember."

"Wait! What are you talking about? You know that guy?"

"Yeah...Well...I know of him. He used to come up here all the time, but I haven't seen him in at least a few years."

"What's his name? Where is he from? What's his story?" she asked eagerly before she even realized the words were coming out of her mouth.

"My, my...how the story changes. I thought you didn't care about him?"

Mackenzie remained silent looking for a way to respond that would reaffirm her original argument. She must have failed because after a minute of no comeback Julie spoke again.

"His name is James. He is from New York City, but

I don't know what he is up to these days because his family lives here now."

"Well, cute or not, I think he is nothing but rude."

"Ah, so you admit you think he is cute?" Julie asked.

"What, no!" she protested. "I didn't say that! You're twisting my words to fit your side of this. I said he is rude. That's all I meant."

"Whatever. What makes him so rude?"

"I have had two interactions with him so far, and in both situations that is the impression I was left with. The first time I ran into him, literally, I bumped into him while I was running. I apologized and got nothing more than a horrible attitude in return. He just strikes me as a jerk."

"Maybe he had a bad day or something," Julie countered. "You're going to judge someone off one brief encounter."

"No, now I'm judging him off of two. The way he acted tonight was absurd."

"He was trying to protect you, isn't that obvious. I'm sure he did it as a way to get to meet you or something. I still say it was hot and you should be flattered."

Mackenzie had enough of the conversation and went home. As far as she was concerned they were all ridiculous. Chad for thinking he owned her and could treat her the way that he did. James for thinking she was weak and trying to be her *savior*. But worst of all was Julie for falling for all of it and giving her such a hard time. She just wanted to go to sleep and forget that it all had even happened.

The next day she woke up late and had to rush through the start of her day. She did some work on her computer and then got ready to go down to the classroom at the church and get things set-up. She usually liked to take care of things early. Although she was only a couple hours behind her regular schedule, she felt as if she was going to end up not being prepared.

When she got into town she went straight to the church. Her classroom was downstairs, but being such a small building she had to go through the main doors to get to the basement. When she walked in through the back of the church she saw someone sitting in a middle pew all alone. From her point of view it seemed like they were just kind of starring off into space. She thought it was a little strange. It was rare for anyone to be in the church at this time, and whenever there was it was just someone off to the side saying a quiet prayer or lighting a candle. She kept to her task at hand and went down the back steps to prepare her classroom for the next day.

By the time she had finished what she was doing she had been downstairs for just short of an hour. On her way out she came up the stairs and blindly turned the corner towards the door, head buried in the floor, and she slammed into someone. Before she even looked up she began to apologize for her clumsiness, but before she got the words out someone else spoke.

"We have got to stop meeting like this," the voice said.

She looked up. "You!" she said. "What are you doing here?"

It was James. He had been the person sitting in the pew when she came in, and he was still there, almost an hour later. Her mind became flooded with thoughts. *Why is he here? Did he follow me? Was he waiting for me? What is with this guy, why doesn't he get it?* She was caught off guard and wanted an explanation. Before giving him a chance to answer her first question she threw out another as if it were some sort of poorly planned interrogation.

"Are you looking for me? What do you want?"

"Looking for you?" he repeated with a confused tone. "I was not looking for you. How would I have even known you would be here?"

Hearing it said out loud she knew he was right and how self-centered she must have sounded. "Well then," she started again. "If you're not here for me, why are you here?"

"It doesn't matter. Personal reasons. By the way, I'm sorry about last night. I hope your boyfriend is okay." He said as he started to walk for the door.

"Boyfriend?!" she yelped. "He is *not* my boyfriend."

"Oh, I heard differently. And based on the way you responded to my helping you last night it only seemed reasonable that it were true."

"I don't know where you heard that, but I assure you it is not the case. We dated years ago, but it didn't even last a month. It was constantly on again off again and just wasn't worth it."

"Either way, I am sorry. I'm not the type of guy that goes out looking for a fight. I really thought you needed help and it didn't seem like anyone else there was going to challenge Chad. I couldn't just sit there while you got hurt."

With that simple explanation of his actions she started to think about everything she had said to Julie the night before. Maybe she had been wrong about him.

She felt a sense of sincerity in his words. She was starting to believe that he had only stepped in to stop Chad. When she thought about it, his actions were very sweet. He put himself in harm's way to help someone that he didn't know. Someone that he had absolutely no obligation to help. If nothing else, that should at least speak for his character. She still believed that she would have been okay without his intervening, but she now saw what he did for her from another perspective.

She invited him to sit down with her. They took a pew in the back of the church and spoke quietly, despite the fact that they were the only ones in the building. It just felt natural considering where they were.

"So, what is it you are doing here?" James asked her.

"I volunteer here."

"And what exactly does that mean?" he asked again.

"I teach a class downstairs. During the mass the little kids can come down and we draw pictures and explain things in a way they can understand it. After the mass it's mostly tutoring for kids that are falling behind or having trouble in school. Now that the school year is over the classes get a lot smaller, but we still have some kids with different types of learning disabilities come in to work on basic reading skills and stuff like that."

"Wow! That is both impressive and unexpected."

"What is so unexpected about it? Do I seem like the type of person that doesn't care about anyone else?" she asked while turning her body towards the front of the church and crossing her arms to show she was insulted.

"No, no. I'm sorry, that's not what I meant at all. It's just that you don't see people our age doing stuff like that too often."

"And that is exactly the type of thing I hope to change one day. Now, I've told you why I am here, but you still haven't told me why you are."

"I told you, it's personal."

"Come on, I won't tell," she said in a playful voice.

"I come here every week around this time. My mother used to love this church before she passed away and...I guess I just feel close to her when I am here."

"Oh, I am so sorry. That is personal," she said looking very embarrassed. "I didn't mean to pry."

"No, it's fine. It was a long time ago now."

If his explanation of the fight didn't make her realize she was wrong about him that certainly did. It became clear that there was so much more to him than that initial rudeness she encountered. Now she saw a kindness in him that she never expected. They spoke for almost another hour before she told him she had to go. She was enjoying their conversation so much that she didn't even realize she was a half hour late to meet Julie.

"When can I see you again?" he asked.

"I don't know. We'll have to see about that, won't we?" she responded with a smirk and walked out of the church.

Nine

Jerry woke up knowing it was going to be a hard day. Last year he didn't even leave the house. In fact, he spent most of the day in bed. He promised himself he wouldn't do that again. This year was going to be different. He had come up with an idea. A way that would honor and remember her life the way she would have wanted.

"Boys, let's go. We've got a lot to do today," he yelled towards their bedroom.

He started to cook her favorite breakfast. He wasn't a very good cook, but it wasn't anything too fancy. That was one of the things he loved about her. She always favored the simple things. The smell of bacon and eggs swept through the small house filling every room with its aroma of deliciousness. The sweet fragrance of the fresh cinnamon rolls still in the oven lingered not far behind. He closed his eyes and took a slow, deep breath as if taking it into his soul. It reminded him of her. Of the times she was there. He could almost feel her next to him in the kitchen just as it was only a few years ago. He could see her at the stove, scrambling the eggs and stealing bits of bacon when she thought no one was looking. The way she would set the table with the cinnamon rolls in the shape of a smiley face, or a heart, or some other picture the kids would find amusing. She loved to cook, but breakfast was definitely her favorite meal.

"Hey Dad, that smells great," Ryan said.

With that he flinched and was snapped back into reality. "Oh hey, thanks," he said, hoping his son didn't see him jump. "Where is your brother?" he asked.

"You know him, still trying to pull himself out of bed."

"James," he yelled, "Let's go. Food's going to get cold."

Unlike his brother, when James walked into the kitchen he did so in a way that resembled the movements of the undead. His hair was disheveled, his clothes a wrinkled mess, and he dragged his feet behind him as if they were too heavy to lift. He went straight to the pot of coffee on the counter, poured it into a tall mug, and gulped it down. It wasn't until after he finished his first cup that he even spoke a word.

"So what's the deal with the eggs?" he asked.

"You know how much your mother loved a homemade breakfast. What better day to make one than today?"

They all ate their breakfast in relative silence. He certainly didn't expect it to be easy, however, now he had no choice but to admit to himself that it was more awkward than he had thought it would be.

"Your mother would have liked this," he said to break the silence. "All of us eating breakfast together as a family."

"You remember when we used to do this all the time with her?" Ryan asked.

"I do. Those were good times," Jerry responded. "I miss them every day."

"Me too."

Jerry looked over at James, who had been ignoring everything that was being said. His head was down and he was pushing his eggs around the plate. It was clear he wasn't comfortable with the topic of conversation. In an attempt to deliver his son from his apparent discomfort he stopped talking, stood up, and dropped his plate into the sink.

"Alright guys, clean up and go get dressed, we have a lot to do today."

Without any argument they did as they were told, not knowing what else their father had planned. Once they arrived at their destination it became clear that they should have known where they were going. Without a word he climbed out of the truck and headed towards her headstone. He heard someone else get out and move quickly behind him to catch up. Without looking back he knew that it was Ryan who followed. He didn't really expect James to get out of the truck. His youngest son caught up to him at her grave and stood next to him, very still, and awkwardly silent. They bowed their heads together and Jerry started with a prayer.

"Eternal rest grant unto her, O Lord; and let perpetual light shine upon her. May she rest in peace. Amen."

As he finished he could see Ryan begin to shed a tear, despite his efforts to hold it back. He knew how hard it must be for his kids, and at Ryan's age, crying was a social taboo that he felt would look like weakness. He reached up and rested his hand on his son's shoulder to console him. Instead, Ryan stiffened his back, wiped his face and walked off back to the truck.

Jerry turned his attention back to the spot where his wife was laid to rest. He crouched down, resting his weight on the headstone and spoke directly to the grass at the base of the stone.

"Don't let that bother you, dear. You know how it is to be that age. James is here, too, he stayed in the truck. This is all still real hard on him. He won't admit it to anyone, but he really misses you. We all miss you.

"I can't believe today makes two years now. It's not fair. We still had so much to do together. We still had so many plans. I hope you are happy with how our boys are growing up. I'm doing my best, trying to raise them the way you would have wanted. It's not always easy, I'd be lying to you if I said it was, but they are good kids. They're more and more like you every day. I guess we got lucky with that one, huh?" he said with a laugh.

"Well, we have to get going. I'm taking the boys down to the salvage yard. There are a few things we have to look at down there. I love you, Kate, I'll be back soon." He stood up, kissed the top of the headstone and walked back to the truck.

When he got in the truck he turned to James. "Do you want to go out there?" he asked. "Maybe you want to talk to her alone."

"I'm good," James said.

"You sure?"

"I said I'm good. Can we just go please?" he snapped and then turned away from his father and looked out the window.

He continued to stare out without a word until he saw where his father was taking them. He didn't see how it fit into the obvious theme of the day and he found himself rather interested.

"What are we doing here?" he asked as they drove passed the aisles of endless garbage.

To their right were piles old refrigerators that were torn to pieces and falling apart. On their left were air conditioners that were obviously ransacked for any working parts. As they continued to drive they reached an area that resembled a parking lot. It was littered with countless rows of broken down, rusted old cars. Some missing doors, others with the hoods left open. Still moving deeper into this graveyard of metal they stopped in a section that was mostly boats scattered around a field. Jerry stopped the truck and got out to speak with the owner. He was an older man who stood there as if he were waiting for them. He had gray hair and wore a pair of ratty overalls on top of a flannel shirt.

"Hey there, Tony," Jerry said as he shook the man's hand. "Thanks for letting us take a look through what you've got."

"Aint no problem at'all. I sifted through some of em myself. I think what yer lookin fer is in da back."

"Okay, I guess that's where we'll start then. Thanks again."

They headed towards the back of the yard where there were rows of old boats. They continued on to the end of the section and found three pontoon boats separated from the rest. The first one they saw was twenty footer and seemed to be pretty much intact. The next was a little bigger, twenty-two feet, and also seemed to be almost complete with the exception of the steering console. The last, and largest at twenty-four feet, at first glance appeared to be in the worst of shape.

"What's the deal with these?" James asked.

"One of these is going to be our next project," Jerry replied. "Your mother always wanted a pontoon boat, so, I figure the three of us can do it together."

"But these are junk..."

"I think it's an awesome idea," Ryan said, jumping into the conversation and cutting his brother off. "We can totally do this."

"You guys are both crazy. Look at these things."

"Hey," Jerry said, "before either of you get too ahead of yourselves let's do just that. Let's look at our choices and see if there is anything we can work with."

They all agreed and started their more detailed inspection. When they examined the first one they noticed that the bench seats were eaten through and had been the obvious home to a family of mice for quite some time. That wasn't the worst part. They expected to have to do some upholstery work. What ruled that one out was when they looked underneath it. All the wood decking was rotted out and needed replacing.

As they moved on, the next one appeared to be half-way decent. The seats obviously needed new fabric covers from sitting outside for so long, but besides that they were in pretty good shape. The floorboards were sturdy and even the carpet was pretty salvageable. The railing looked like it needed to be cleaned up a bit as it had some spots of rust, but if that was the worst of it, they found their boat. James climbed under it again and called to his father.

"Hey Dad, you might want to see this."

As Jerry joined his son under the boat he thought he saw what his son was talking about. There was a buildup of rust where the pontoons met the frame of the boat. When he rubbed away at it he saw it was more than just surface rust, it had eaten through the metal. The pontoon was separating from the frame.

"You talking about those connections there? We can re-weld that. That's not a problem."

"That's not what I'm talking about Dad. Over there." James pointed to a big hole on one of the pontoons. "We can't fix that."

"Well then, I guess that rules this one out."

"What did I tell you, garbage," James said.

Ryan was already looking at the third one when James and his father were still under the second. "Hey guys, this one looks pretty good," he said.

"That one is nothing but a shell," James said back while he was climbing out from under the one he had just been inspecting.

"No really, I'm serious. I know it doesn't look that good from there, and it doesn't have anything on it, but just take a look. The fence railing can be cleaned up and the dents can be knocked out. Now look under here, the pontoons are in good shape, no signs of any rust and there isn't a bit of rot in the floorboards. I think this one is our best bet."

As his brother and father looked around they couldn't find anything wrong with what was left of this boat.

"It will cost a fortune to buy all new seats for this thing," James said.

"Not if we buy the seats from the one with the bad pontoons," Jerry said. "They are still decent. If we make covers for them they'll be as good as new."

He went to talk to Tony about buying the stripped down twenty-four footer as well as the seats, and when he came back he was pulling a trailer. He backed it up in front of the wooden frame that held the boat off the ground and lined the supports up with the pontoons. He got out of the truck with some tools, handed them to his kids and told them to start taking the seats out of the other boat. While they did that he hooked the trailers crank to the front of the twenty-four footer and pulled it from its stand. When James and Ryan were done lifting the seats from the other boat they loaded them into the bed of the truck and they headed home with their new project.

Ten

A week had gone by since James had seen Mackenzie and he found himself thinking about her a lot. A lot more than even made sense. He found himself hung up on the way they left off at the church, and that comment she made when he asked if he could see her again. He heard her words over and over again in his head. *We'll have to see about that, won't we?* He kept asking himself what it meant. Then he thought about the smirk she made when she said it. At least he thought it was a smirk. *Was it something she meant for me to notice?* he thought. *Did it mean anything at all?* All the thoughts swimming through his mind were driving him crazy. He hardly knew this girl, in fact, they only had that one decent conversation, but there was something about her. He couldn't quite figure out what it was, but he felt as if there was some sort of connection between them. All he knew was if he didn't try to see her again there was a good chance it would end up being one of those lifelong 'what ifs'.

That Saturday he woke up earlier than he normally

did. He showered quickly and put a little more thought into his outfit than he typically would. He jumped in his truck and headed into town. He stopped by the deli for his usual egg sandwich and cup of coffee, then sat on his tailgate and finished both before heading around the corner to the church. He got there two hours before normal and hoped to see her there. He sat in his usual pew and faced the front of the church, but with every creek of the old building he found himself eagerly turning around towards the door. He sat there longer than he ever had before, but she never showed up.

Maybe she knew I would be here, he thought to himself, *it's obvious she's not interested*. He heard another creek in the floor, this time followed by the sound of the door opening, and again he spun around. It was just an older woman coming in with a rosary wrapped around her hand. *See, she's not coming!* his inner voice yelled at him. *Maybe she just doesn't have anything to set up for her class this week*, he argued back at himself. He stayed patient and waited for a while longer, but eventually he came to admit that it didn't seem like she was coming and he left.

Slightly upset, he spent the rest of the day trying to keep himself occupied. When he got back to the house Ryan was at the computer looking up pictures of pontoon boats. He had compiled a collection of photos with the different features and accessories that he wanted to include on their new boat. After that they went outside and spent a good part of what was left of the afternoon tearing up the old carpet from the base of the boat. They rolled it up and threw it in front of the house for garbage pickup. There was no shade over the spot behind the garage where the boat was parked and with the sun beating down on them the entire time the heat was overwhelming. When they finished their work they spent the rest of the day swimming in the water off the dock to cool off.

The next morning James slept in later than he had planned to. By the time he got out of bed it was eleven o'clock and when he went to the kitchen for his morning cup of coffee it seemed like no one else was home. He sat quietly at the table and read the paper as he slowly sipped from his mug. He decided to makes some breakfast, but when he went to the refrigerator he found a note hanging there from his father.

James,

We didn't want to wake you, but we are going to the river to do some fly fishing. We went to the diner for some breakfast and then we are going to the general store in town to get some new flies. If you want to join meet us in town.

Dad

He shook his head, "Why would they go down to the river to go fly fishing when they have the lake right here?" he said to himself despite there being no one there to hear him.

He knew they loved to go fly fishing, and the Beaverkill River was the best place to do it. He always preferred just fishing off the boat, but he figured he didn't have any other plans for the day so he called Billy to see if he was interested. Of course he was. Billy never missed an opportunity to go fishing and they made plans to meet in town before finding his family. He got his gear together, threw it in the back of the truck, and headed out.

When he got into town he didn't see Billy and he noticed his father's truck wasn't in front of the general store. Seeing how Billy always ran late for everything, he figured he would do a quick lap through the parking lot of the diner to see if his father's truck was there. It wasn't. He knew they must already be fishing and figured they would meet them at their favorite spot under the bridge off old route 17. As he turned the corner back towards the center of town he just happened to look down the sidewalk. There she was. Mackenzie. She was walking down the street with Julie and they were coming towards him while he sat at the red light. When the light turned green he pulled over and waited for them to get closer. As they walked past the side of the truck he leaned over to open the window.

"You need a ride?" he asked, catching them off guard. He saw them jump a bit, but he was pretty sure he caught a slight smile on Mackenzie's face when she saw it was him.

"Hey there," Mackenzie said as she leaned against the door and slightly in the window. "We're actually good. We're not going that far."

With Julie standing slightly behind her he figured he had to take advantage of the opportunity in front of him.

"Well hey I was thinking. I'd like to see you again. Maybe I could take you to dinner tonight?"

"I don't think so," she said. "I don't even know you."

"Well if you don't give me the chance to take you out how could you possibly get to know me?"

She turned around and whispered something to Julie. Julie looked over at him with some type of grin. Or maybe it was a grimace. He couldn't tell. He tried to hear what they were saying but he couldn't. He started to feel a little embarrassed and self-conscious, then, Mackenzie turned around again.

"Here's the deal, what are you doing now?"

"Now? Not much, I was just going to meet up with my friend Billy.

She looked back at Julie who nodded with a little smile. He saw it clearly this time. It was definitely a smile.

"That's perfect," she said. "We missed breakfast this morning and we are on our way to the diner. Call your friend and you can meet us there."

"Sure," he said, knowing Billy wouldn't really like this sudden change of plans, but not wanting to miss this opportunity. "We'll see you in a few minutes."

It wasn't long before Billy showed up and pulled into the parking space next to James' truck in front of the general store. They both acknowledged each other and rolled down their windows.

"Hey, man," James said. "Let's shoot over to the diner first."

"Sounds like you're buying, huh?"

"Yeah, I'm buying. Meet me over there."

"No problem," he said as they backed out of their spaces and drove up to the diner.

When they walked in the front doors James looked around to see where the girls were sitting. Billy noticed his eyes fixed in their direction and grabbed him by the arm before he even got passed the front counter.

"Did you bring me here to meet up with them?" he asked sharply.

"Come on, dude, it wasn't my original plan. I bumped into them while I was waiting for you and it just came up."

"I'm out. I came here to go fishing, not play wingman for you while you get crushed by some north shore girl."

"Bill it's not like that. She's not like that. It's just lunch. Besides, Julie made it pretty clear she wanted you to come. It almost seemed like she has a thing for you."

"What are you talking about? I don't know her and she doesn't know me. She's north shore and I'm not. That's all there is to it."

"Look, I know how you feel about them. Can you just do this for me? Just this one time?"

Billy looked at James, then up at the table where the girls where, then back at James again. "Just this once," he responded. "But if they start acting all snotty, and they probably will, I'm out of here and you're on your own."

"You got it. Thanks, man," James said and he turned to walk to the table.

They spent the next hour and a half sitting there, James and Mackenzie on one side of the table, and Billy and Julie on the other. At first Billy made it clear that he didn't want to be there, but Julie didn't even attempt to conceal her flirting and he loosened up a bit. James and Billy joked around and talked about when they were younger and all the things they had done to get themselves into trouble. The girls laughed at their stories and made it clear they were having a good time.

At the end of lunch they walked the girls back to their cars at the church. As Mackenzie was getting into her jeep James repeated the question he asked before the last time they said goodbye.

"When can I see you again?"

"I don't know. We'll have to see about that, won't we?" she responded again with a giggle and the same smirk she gave him the last time.

He wasn't about to let her go like that again so he responded immediately. "Let me take you to dinner tonight."

She stopped, turning her body back to face James from the driver's seat. "I've never really been the dinner and a movie kind of girl. There's a carnival in Livingston Manor tonight that our church is running with our sister church there. I'll be there early to help set some stuff up, how about you meet me there at around nine-ish at the ticket booth."

"Sounds like a plan, I'll see you then."

"What about you?" Julie asked Billy. "You going to come, too?"

"I don't know, maybe. I'm not making any promises."

"Well then, maybe I'll see you there."

"Maybe…"

After they all said their goodbyes the girls drove off and James turned to Billy. "What the hell was that, man?"

"What?" he asked as if he really didn't know what James was talking about.

"Maybe…Not making any promises…Dude, she's into you and you're completely missing it. Just look at the way she was flirting with you."

"She playing a game, and to be honest, I'm not interested. It was fun at the diner, but I'm not looking to make it a regular thing."

James told him how ridiculous he was being and left.

That night he got to the carnival at ten minutes before nine and walked through it until he found the ticket booth which was placed near the center of everything. As he got close he noticed Mackenzie wasn't there so he stood next to it. After a while of waiting he asked the woman in the booth if she knew where he could find her.

"I think she's by the games in the back. That way," she said while she pointed, "towards the booths to the right."

As he walked around he looked into the booths wondering what could have kept her, and then he saw her. She was at the ring toss booth helping the little kids throw their plastic rings, which were obviously bigger than the ones most people had to use, around the necks of the bottles. They were letting the kids throw until they got a ringer. He stood there watching as she got excited for each child, despite the fact that they obviously set it up in their favor, and he was amazed at how good she was with them. She gave each one a prize and then she looked at her watch. He saw as she fixed her hair a bit and then hurried in the direction of the ticket booth. He doubled back and got to the ticket booth before her, not to let on that he had been watching her.

"Hey, there you are," he said in a joking tone as he saw her walking up to the booth. "I thought you were going to stand me up."

"I'm sorry," she said. "I got tied up helping some

people."

"Not a problem. What do you want to do first?"

At first they just walked around the carnival and talked for a while. Along the way they stopped and played a few games. She beat him in the water gun races, but he restored his pride at the milk bottle toss. He was armed with three hard balls to knock down the bottles but he accomplished the task with only one, winning her an oversized stuffed monkey. The next game they played was one he was sure he could win her a prize from. They were each given a rifle and with the preloaded bb's they had to shoot down as many of the moving ducks and targets as they could. He let out five consecutive shots at the lower set of targets and the pinging sound of metal rang out with each one. He paused and turned to her.

"This is nothing, might as well pick out what you want now."

She didn't respond. She simply smiled at him and aimed her rifle at the targets that were quickly moving across the top row. She let out six shots, each one finding its intended target perfectly.

"Where did you learn that?" he asked.

"I don't know. Must be beginners luck," she said in a teasing voice before she shot down four more targets from the top row.

He quickly faced the game again and now both of them were shooting simultaneously and knocking down the targets. When most of the targets were down there were two metal ducks left gliding across the top row. She fired and knocked one down with a loud ping. He laughed as he fired his rife, but there was no sound. He missed. He couldn't believe it. He missed. She beat him at shooting. She chose a large light blue teddy bear and handed it to him.

"Now I won you a prize," she said.

He simply laughed and gratefully accepted it from her. As they made their way back towards the entrance they saw an old photo booth and Mackenzie insisted on taking a picture in it. They went in and James slipped the money into the bill slot. A light blinked and then the camera shot four pictures. It dispensed the string of photos and Mackenzie tore it in half, giving two of them to James and keeping the other two for herself.

"Something to remember tonight by," she said.

When they stepped out of the photo booth someone stepped out in front of them. Three people actually.

"Well now, what do we have here?" they heard from the one in the center of the group. "Are you really hanging out with this guy?"

"Leave us alone, Chad." Mackenzie said firmly.

He didn't respond to her. Instead he turned his attention to James. "So, mister sucker punch, you think you could take me now? Now that I'm looking you right in the face and can see it coming?"

"Listen, I'm not looking for any problems. We were just leaving."

Chad took a step closer to James and went nose to nose with him. "What's the matter, afraid to fight me now?" he asked and then shoved him backwards.

"I'm not going to fight you," James said loudly.

"Well that's too bad because I have every intention of fighting you," he said as he moved towards him again.

"What's going on over there!" yelled a voice from behind Chad that caused him to stop his advance on

James. He looked over his shoulder to identify the source. Seeing Father O'Reilly he turned back to James. "You're lucky this time," he said and then reached a hand out towards Mackenzie. "Come on, I'll take you home."

"No!" she said. "I'm here with James, he'll take me home."

"Seriously? Come on I'm taking you home."

"No you're not," she said firmly and reached out for James to take her hand. They walked passed Chad and his friends, Derek and Kurt, and headed for the parking lot.

Mackenzie had gone to the carnival with Julie, who was still working in one of the booths, so they got into James' truck. On the drive back to town James apologized for what had just happened and restated that he wasn't the type to go out looking for a fight.

"You did the right thing," she said. "He's just a jerk."

When they got to the north shore area she directed him to her house. He pulled into the driveway but was greeted by a locked gate. She leaned over him to reach out his window and type the code into the keypad and the gate opened. He drove up to the front door and put the truck in park. They sat there awkwardly for a minute until she broke the silence.

"I had a lot of fun tonight," she said. "More than I've had in a long time."

"So did I, when can we go out again?"

This time instead of teasing him she gave him her phone number and said, "Anytime, hopefully soon." She leaned forward and kissed him on the cheek.

Before he realized what was happening she was out

the door and walking into her house.

Eleven

Billy knocked on the door and stood there longer than he had expected waiting for James to answer. After a few minutes of no response he rang the doorbell and knocked again, this time louder than he did before. There was still no answer. Knowing James was home he took out his cell phone and called him while he knocked on the door a third time. After a ring and a half the phone went to voicemail so he knew he had to be awake. He pounded on the door again.

"Come on, wake up. It's nearly noon," he yelled. "Open the door."

Finally James appeared in the doorway. "What are you doing here?" he asked. "Shouldn't you be at work?"

"It's my day off. Come out to the truck and give me a hand with something."

Billy could plainly see he didn't want to help him with whatever it was he had out there by the expression on his face.

"Come on, man," James said. "This is one of the first times I've had the house to myself since my father made me start working with him." Work was starting to slow down a bit and they didn't need a three man crew so he got to take the day off.

"I'm pretty sure you're going to appreciate what it is I have to show you. Humor me."

James threw on a pair of sneakers and reluctantly followed Billy out to the end of the driveway. In the bed of Billy's truck all he could see was a large bulge under a blue tarp and he definitely had a growing sense of curiosity at this point.

When they got closer to the truck Billy hoped up into the bed. "Are you ready for this?" he asked. "I was talking to your father and he told me that you guys were looking for a new motor for the boat you just got. Well…" He flipped the tarp over the side of the truck revealing a 250 horsepower outboard motor that looked like it was still in pretty good shape.

"Where the hell did you get that?" James asked him.

"Consider it a donation," he said with a little laugh.

"What does that mean? You take this off a boat down the road or something?"

"No, it's nothing like that. One of our boats at the parks department got damaged so bad they couldn't fix it."

"And they just let you take the motor?"

"Well, not exactly. Usually they keep parts from the messed up boats, but under certain circumstances it's not worth it to them. This motor is about ten or twelve years old. There are too many hours on it for them to stick it on another boat so I was able to cash in some of my comp time for it."

"You didn't have to do that."

"Don't worry about it. Where else would you get a deal like that on a motor in as good of shape as this one?"

"Thanks a lot man. I can't tell you how cool this is."

"That's not all," Billy said.

"What are you talking about? There's more?"

With that Billy moved up farther to the front of the bed and pulled back the rest of the tarp. He revealed a steering console. It was a little beat up, but nothing that a little cleaning up couldn't fix.

"All the gauges work. I know that for a fact," Billy said.

"There is no way we can take all this from you. You got all of this from cashing in your comp time?"

"I already told you not to worry about it. Your father told me about how your mother always wanted to do this. I just wanted to help."

"Thanks, man. This means a lot," James said before giving him a serious look. "But that stays between us."

"I know how much you miss her Jim. It kept you away from here for two years. I just wanted to help you do this for her."

There was an awkward silence for a minute before anyone spoke again. "Come on, what do you say we get started on this thing?" James asked.

"You want me to help with this? Really?"

"Of course, we wouldn't have this thing if it weren't for you. Besides, you think I can figure all this out?"

They spent the next hour just laying everything out by the boat. They put the console in the appropriate location on the boat and hooked up the steering cable to it. They ran the cable through the track that was already setup for the old cables. When they were done with that they used the hoist that Billy had on the back of his truck to lift the motor into place. Billy worked the hoist while James guided it into place ensuring the mounting bracket lined up properly. Once it was fastened into place they worked on connecting the steering cable.

After they finished that Billy hooked up the fuel line and started to show James how to wire all the gauges. While they were working Billy asked him about his date with Mackenzie. When James started to tell him how good of a time he had Billy began to mumble something under his breath.

"What's your problem?" James asked.

"It's nothing, never mind."

"You asked me how it went. Now that I am giving you an answer that you obviously didn't want to hear you're going to get all short?"

"I just think you're getting a little ahead of yourself. She is a north shore girl. It's not like it could possibly work out."

"How am I getting ahead of myself?" James responded with a bit of a snap.

"I'm just saying...you can't trust those girls."

"Whatever. She's not like that. I've had enough of this conversation. Let's just stick to the boat for now."

They continued to work in silence until all the gauges appeared to be hooked up properly. The throttle cable was set in place and the lever moved with the appropriate amount of tension. When testing the steering the motor moved with full range of motion. They were satisfied with their work as far as they could test it. In order to run the engine and be sure everything actually worked the way it was supposed to they would still need to get a battery, as well as fill the tank with fuel and put oil in the motor. All things they planned to do soon, but after spending the better part of a day on the boat already they just wanted to relax.

When it came to relaxing Billy had only one favorite way to do that. Fishing. They still had a few hours before it got dark so they grabbed some gear and headed out on James' father's boat. They didn't approach the expedition with much of a strategy, just the desire to cast out their lines and hang out. After being anchored for about twenty minutes in what appeared to be a decent spot, to the best they could tell anyway without the help of the fish finder on Billy's boat, they only got a few nibbles.

"So you got any plans for this weekend?" Billy asked in an attempt to start small talk.

"Actually I do," James responded. "I'm meeting up with Mackenzie on Saturday for the Fourth of July parade in town and then we're going to the firework show together."

"You're really starting to spend a lot of time with this girl," Billy said with a shake of his head.

"And what's the problem with that? Why don't you come with us? I'm sure Julie would like to see you."

"No thanks. You have fun."

"Why are you so against hanging out with them? It wasn't that miserable when we were all at the diner together, was it?" James asked.

"I shouldn't have done it then and I'm not going to do it now," Billy said quietly.

"What is up with you? I know you have some kind of animosity against the people from the north shore, but these two girls haven't been anything but nice."

"Whatever, let's just drop it."

"No, I don't want to drop it this time," James said

in a voice calmer than before. "You are always talking about how much they think they're better than everyone else, and how much they live in their own little world, but I don't see it. They seem fine to me. Mackenzie isn't like that, and I haven't seen anything in Julie to make me think she is either."

"Ha," Billy said sarcastically. "You obviously don't know her that well."

"Well then, why don't you enlighten me?" James asked with a look on his face that showed he expected some half-witted response that didn't really explain anything.

"It started when we were in high school. It was the start of my junior year and Julie was a freshman. I kind of had a thing for her. We hung out a little, you know, mostly at school. We sat at the same lunch table, talked during study hall, that sort of thing. I never came right out and told her how I felt, but she had to have known." Billy paused briefly as if he still wasn't sure he wanted to be saying what he was and James just looked at him quietly. He kept his stare focused on the water and continued. "The north shore was just starting to really develop then into what it is now and I guess she felt she had to establish her reputation to fit in with the richer group that was moving in up there. Before I built up the courage to ask her out she just forgot I existed. Eventually when I tried to say hi to her in the hall she just walked passed me like I wasn't even there. She showed me then how shallow she was. How shallow they all are."

"Hey, man, I had no idea, but that was what…almost four years ago?"

"Yeah, just about I guess. What's your point?"

"My point is exactly that. It was four years ago, that's a pretty long time. Things change with time. People change."

"No, not that much."

"Listen, she blew you off back then and I'm sure that hurt you, but are you really going to hold a grudge forever? Maybe she didn't know you were into her."

"I don't really care," Billy answered.

"If it means anything, from what I saw it seems like she really is interested in you."

"It doesn't. Even if she is, why now? Why after all this time?"

"I'm not telling you to date her, just relax a little. Put your guard down enough that you can at least hang out with us."

"Sorry, Jim, it's just not worth it to me. I can't trust people like that, especially her."

Twelve

On the morning of the Fourth of July James woke up and headed into town to meet up with Mackenzie. Roscoe always had a parade for the holiday, and despite the fact that it was a small parade, in a small town, it always got a pretty good turnout. He met her at the diner, which was starting to become a routine of theirs. They met a while before the parade was scheduled to start so they would have time to get some breakfast first. They drank their coffee, ate their eggs, and talked about a little bit of everything and a lot of nothing. Just like always. As she spoke he just watched her and couldn't help but to think about how comfortable he felt around her. How he really felt like he could tell her anything. It had been a long time since the felt that way, and he couldn't deny that he liked it.

James paid the bill and threw a tip on the table before they made their way outside. They started walking around the corner to Main Street where the parade was going to take place just as they heard the announcer tap on his microphone.

"Testing, testing. 1...2...3," the voice said through the speakers.

They continued to walk down towards the center of the block so they could be sure to see everything. Being that it was a small parade that only went the length of that one block, if they were to stay up at the corner the groups marching would start to break apart when they got to them and they really wouldn't be able to see all that much.

"Ladies and gentlemen, I would like to thank you all for coming out this year," the mayor continued on the microphone as they walked. "We are just about to get started so I hope everyone is ready. We have a great day planned today."

When James and Mackenzie got to the middle of the block he heard someone yelling his name over the sound of the crowd. He stopped to look around when he saw Ryan at the curb line waving his arms in the air.

"James," he yelled again. "Over here, we've got plenty of room."

"I think we're good," James yelled back before he turned to keep walking.

"Is that your brother?" Mackenzie asked.

"Yeah, he's probably up there with my father, too. Let's just find someplace else to sit."

"Oh stop, let's go sit with them. I'd love to meet them."

"There is nothing that special about them, I promise. We don't have to."

"But I want to, come on," she said as she took him by the hand and started to push her way through the crowd towards where Ryan was standing.

Without any further protest he let her drag him

through the crowd that separated them from his family. He couldn't help but think if he were the one pushing on people's arms and trying to fish his way around them he would have never made it to the curb, but her, it was effortless. She simply tapped them on the arm and in a sweet voice said excuse me. Once they turned and saw the beautiful young girl behind them they just stepped out of her way without another word. He was a little taken back by how easy it was for her, but at the same time he felt a little privileged because he was the one in tow behind her.

When they got to the curb Ryan was standing there waiting for them and gave James a pound as he greeted him. His father was sitting in a folding camping chair and stood up as soon as he saw that Mackenzie was with him. James introduced her to his father first, then his brother, and that was when Jerry invited them to stay and watch the parade with them. James quickly told him that he didn't want to get in their way and they could find another place to watch from, but his father insisted. Mackenzie was the one that finally agreed, and once she did there was nothing James could do about it. Jerry offered his seat to her and shot Ryan a look that said he should offer his to his brother. Mackenzie thanked him but refused, and before he could offer any argument she sat down on the curb. James sat next to her, positioning himself between her and his family. He didn't want to stay there. Not because he didn't like his family, but because he was afraid of what they might say or do to embarrass him in front of her. It wasn't because she had more money than them, because he really didn't think she was like that, it was just the way they were. He always believed that his father got a kick out of embarrassing him in front of girls. It never bothered him in the past, but this time was different, he didn't want anything to screw things up.

They only had time for a little basic conversation before the parade started and James was relieved that they hadn't done anything humiliating...yet. As the parade started he saw his father reach down next to his chair and grab something. When he looked to see what he was doing he watched as his father put on his humongous trout hat. James had forgotten about that horrid thing. It's not like his father was the only one wearing one, it kind of went with the theme of the parade, being that the town was nicknamed "Trout Town USA," but how embarrassing.

"Dad, take that ridiculous thing off," James snapped.

"What, everyone's wearing one."

"Come on, Dad, you always gotta find a way to embarrass me don't you?"

Jerry didn't say a word. He just looked at James and started to laugh.

That made him even angrier with his father and snapped at him again. "What are you laughing at?"

Jerry couldn't answer because he was laughing so hard, instead he just pointed at something behind James. When he turned to see what his father was pointing at he saw Mackenzie wearing a big trout hat, too, and mocking the way he was yelling at his father. James right away understood her point. He laughed along with them and apologized to his father.

They watched as the first float came around the corner. It was the same float that the parade was always led by. The giant green bus that was converted to look like a trout. It slowly drove by with the banners hanging on both sides that said "TROUT TOWN, USA Roscoe, N.Y." and everyone cheered. Behind the giant trout was a float being pulled by a pickup truck that was designed to look like the river. It had mechanical fish jumping in the cardboard water and a man standing in the middle dressed as Uncle Sam wearing waders and flicking around a fly-rod as if he were fishing. Following that was a line of old cars that people were throwing candy from and the children ran into the street to pick it up. There was a slight pause in the parade after that and then the Boy Scout troop marched by. As they passed, two little boys that were probably about nine years old came running from their troop yelling Mackenzie's name. They ran up to her and hugged her, almost knocking her over, and then they ran back to their group just as quickly.

"What was that all about?" James asked.

"They come to my class at the church. They are the sweetest little boys. They just needed a little help with their reading."

James thought that was the most adorable thing, and he grew even more attracted to her, if that was even possible. He knew she had the class at the church, but this was the first time he saw any part of it. Those kids really loved her. She must have really been making a difference in their lives.

His thoughts were interrupted by the blaring of the fire trucks that followed the Boy Scouts. The two engines and the ladder truck of the town's volunteer fire department passed by and the spectators cheered again. Following them was the float from the North Shore

Homeowners Association. There were three men on the back of a decorated flatbed truck and some younger kids sitting around them near the edge. One of the men was Chad's father. James recognized him right away, and even if he hadn't, that ridiculous president's sash he was wearing would have given it away. Next to him was Chad. James hoped he wouldn't see them, but sure enough, just as they passed, his eyes landed dead on them. He turned to the third man that was on the truck, a man that James had never seen before, and said something to him while pointing in their direction. James looked over at Mackenzie and noticed that she was looking away, obviously avoiding making eye contact. James thought it was strange, but thought it better to leave it alone for now.

When the parade ended Jerry invited them back to the house for a barbecue he had planned. There weren't going to be that many people. Ryan was going to be there with some of his friends and besides that Jerry only invited two others. James told his father that he had other plans, but they had to go back to the house anyway, so they would see them there. When they got back to the house his father had already been setting things up. James saw his father trying to move the picnic table and ran over to give him a hand.

"You should stick around for a while, you're a good influence. He has never jumped in to help like this without being asked," Jerry said as they carried the table passed Mackenzie.

James shot his father a dirty look and Mackenzie giggled. After they helped set up the rest of the stuff his father had to get together Ryan talked Mackenzie into staying to eat something. James reminded her that he had plans for them and she assured him that they would get to his plans as soon as they were done eating. She was having fun getting to know his family, and as much as he was worried about it earlier in the day, he was becoming a little more comfortable with it. He liked that they liked her, but even more, he liked that she liked them. They weren't embarrassing him. She didn't think they were overdoing it. There was nothing like that. It just felt, natural.

By the time they finished eating, and Jerry finished telling stories about when James was little, they got on with their original plans.

"You mind giving me a hand with something in the garage?" James asked her.

"So that was your plan all along? Bring me here to help clean the garage?" she asked with a laugh.

"No, we just need to get something and I can't carry it by myself."

He took her to the back corner of the garage where there is something big under a heavy blanket. James pulled the cover off and revealed an old style wooden rowboat.

"This is beautiful," she said when she saw it.

"Thank you," he said through his breath as he pulled it away from the wall and positioned the bow towards her. He grabbed the oars from the wall and laid them inside the boat. "You think you can grab that end and carry it out?"

She reached down and lifted the front. It wasn't a very heavy boat, but he could see that it wasn't the most comfortable task for her. When they got outside of the garage James yelled for Ryan to come help him carry it the rest of the way down to the dock and Mackenzie followed along.

"You're really going to take her out in that death-trap?" Jerry said with a laugh as they walked passed him.

James shot his father a look that only made him laugh harder. When they got to the dock James lowered it into the water with the help of his brother. Holding onto the dock he stepped down into the older looking, beautifully made vessel and reached out a hand to help Mackenzie in. She took a seat at the stern so she could face him as he rowed. He pushed away from the dock and began to row away from the house.

"Be careful out there, I hope you make it back," Jerry yelled jokingly as they rowed away.

"Why does he keep saying stuff like that?" Mackenzie asked.

"Don't worry, there's nothing wrong with this boat. It's probably one of the strongest boats on this lake. I haven't used it in a while, but I still trust it, even more than that old Sea Ray that my grandfather left us. I love this boat, and I love the peace that comes along with being on it."

"Well then, why does your father say those things about it?"

"Honestly?" he paused before continuing as if trying to choose his words carefully. "That's probably because it did go down once. Well, it didn't really go down, but it was taking on water and he had to come out here and get me and my grandfather. It was our first time launching it and we only got a little ways out when it started to go down. My father came out to get us and we towed it back to the house. He hasn't let me forget it ever since."

"So you almost went down in this thing? Why are we using it now? How do you know you can trust it?"

My grandfather and I did it together. It only took on water that day because when I sealed it I guess I rushed through the job because I really wanted it to be done. I learned that day that sometimes you need to be patient. To get the absolute best out of something you have to take your time and put the work in. When we got back to the house that day we let the boat dry, then stripped it down and resealed it. I took my time that time and did it right. I've never had a problem with it since."

"You built this boat?" she asked with a surprised tone. "Seriously?"

"Yeah, of course my grandfather did a lot of the work at first, but once I got the hang of it he made me do more and more of it."

"That is amazing, it's so beautiful. I can't believe you made this."

"Thank you."

James continued to row until they reached a tiny cove not too far from his house. It was a rather secluded area with no other boats around. He stopped rowing and without the use of an anchor he allowed the boat to just float and drift in the area.

"This is one of my favorite places on the lake," he said. "Not a lot of other boats ever come over here."

"What's that building over there?" she asked pointing towards the shore.

"That's a pretty cool story actually," James said. "My grandfather told me all about it once. That is actually an old convent."

"A convent? It looks like a boathouse."

"Well yeah, it's both actually. The nuns lived upstairs and every day at noon the bells in that tower there would ring. When they rang the nuns would row out onto the lake in one of those real long rowing team boats and just go, in the whole habit and everything. An hour later the bells would ring again and they would row back into the boathouse. My grandfather told me that was the only time the nuns were really seen out here on the lake, but they closed the convent sometime in the 80's."

"That is a pretty cool story. I never even really noticed the building nevertheless knew all that."

They sat and floated in the cove for what seemed like a long time and they talked about a lot of things. It was starting to get a little dark and there was always a firework display over the lake. They knew they would be able to see it well from where they were and not be surrounded by other boats so they had no intentions of moving. As they talked James told her he had a confession to make. He told her that he was really enjoying the time they were spending together and that after the first time in the church he felt like he had to see her again. He told her that in order to ensure seeing her again he went to the church that next Saturday earlier than he usually did and waited there, hoping they would *bump* into each other. He continued to tell her that when she never showed up he left very disappointed. When he finished talking she simply responded by laughing.

"I don't see what's so funny," he said.

"What's so funny is the reason I didn't show up. The reason you didn't see me at the church that day is simple, I wanted to be sure that we saw each other, too, so I went to the church later than I usually do. The first time we met it was a completely random thing that I went to the church that late. When you said you were always there at that time I figured that would be the surest way to see you again. When you didn't show up I was probably just as disappointed as you were."

They both laughed about the situation and then positioned some life jackets on the floor of the boat so they could lie down and hold one another. As they talked and it grew darker she started to ask James about school, and philosophy, and life. She then asked him about his plans for the future and what he wants to do with his life. When people asked him that question he usually said he was going to discover some eternal truth and write about it, or that he was going to teach the philosophy that he found answers in, or sometimes he would just deflect the question all together by changing the subject, but this time he froze up.

"I don't have the slightest idea," he finally admitted. "All I know is that I don't ever want to come back to this place again."

She was a little confused by his response. "What's wrong with this place?" she asked. "It is absolutely beautiful here."

"That has nothing to do with it," he said.

"So then what is it?"

Again he became very quiet. He stared off into the darkening sky and just as she thought he was going to ignore the question he started to speak.

"It's not so much what this place is as much as what it represents. To me this place used to mean so much. It was a place where I could get away from the crazy life of the city. A place where I tried new things for the first time. Where I grew and learned things that shaped me into who I would become. But now…" he paused again as he fought a tear he felt about to fall. "Now, this place represents nothing but loss. My family lives here because my father lost everything. His business. His home. Everything.

"This place took my mother from me, too, I don't know if you know that. One weekend my father, Ryan, and I were all up here, just like we usually were, and my mother wanted to surprise us. She came up without telling anyone. As she came around the big bend there just off Lake Road, the one with the wooden cross on the tree, another car came whipping around the bend from the opposite direction. The two cars smacked mirrors and as a result my mother lost control and ended up going off the cliff. She died that day. I don't see any reason to come back here and constantly be reminded of all that pain."

She sat quietly, not really knowing what to say, and then the fireworks started. James was a little relieved they didn't have to talk anymore and just held her. When the fireworks were over he slowly rowed back to the house, staying close to the shoreline and using it as his guide. The whole way back she didn't speak. She didn't say a word until they got out of the boat.

As they stood on the dock she turned to him and looked deep into his eyes. "Will you meet me tomorrow morning at six o'clock?" she asked. "I know it's early, but there is something I really have to show you."

He agreed and then drove her back into town where her car was parked. The whole ride was uncomfortably quiet. He asked her what they were going to do so early and she told him to just dress comfortably, preferably in clothes that he wouldn't mind getting dirty. He was confused, but he agreed. She reminded him to be ready by six, then they kissed and she climbed out of the truck.

Thirteen

When she got home she was still shocked by what he had told her. Julie said that he hadn't been here in years, but she never said why. She called Julie right away and explained to her that she planned to bring James to the trails in the morning. She didn't want to exclude her friend from something they had been doing together for a while, so she made it clear that if she still wanted to come she was more than welcome.

Julie was quiet for a minute before she finally spoke. "Are you sure you really want to do this Kenz?" she asked while trying not to sound worried.

"What do you mean?" she asked with an almost defensive tone.

"You know what I mean." "You have never invited a guy to the trails before. Never. Are you sure you want to invite this guy that far into your life."

"James isn't like any other guy I have ever met. There is something about him that draws me in. I need him to come to the trails."

"I think it is too soon. I know you guys are hitting it off, but I think you are going a little fast with all this. You have never been the type to fall for a guy this hard this fast."

"I know, and I appreciate your concern, but I have to do this. He opened up to me and now I have to do the same."

"Well, you do what you need to do, but I'm not going to be the third wheel. I'm just going to sleep in for once. I'll see you after."

The next morning she woke up a little bit earlier than she normally would for her Sunday ride. She started to get herself ready, and for the first time ever she took the time to put on a little make-up and pull her hair back into a neat ponytail. Julie was right. She had never invited a guy to the trails before and it was a big deal for her. She put her bike on the back of her jeep and then went to the garage to where Jeremy's old bikes were. She just looked at them for a while. It had been so long since any of them had been used. She convinced herself that bikes were meant to be ridden and that her brother would agree with her, so, she took one that was still in good shape and put it on the jeep, too.

When she pulled up in front of James' house he wasn't there. She waited for five minutes, but it felt much longer as she watched the clock. She hoped he hadn't overslept, or forgotten all together, and just as she was going to call him he came running out the door.

"Six o'clock, huh?" she asked with a smile on her face.

"I'm sorry, it's early…I'm not much of a morning person."

"Don't worry about it. I was just about to call you,

but I was trying to hold off on it because I didn't want to wake your brother or anything."

"It wouldn't have been a problem. I was in the kitchen. But even if I were in the room, that kid could sleep through anything. Back when we lived in the Bronx there was a fire at the house next door once and when the fire department showed up the lights and sirens woke up the entire neighborhood, except Ryan. He slept through the entire thing."

"That's pretty impressive, sometimes I wish I could sleep that well."

"Anyway, what are the plans? I couldn't help but notice the bikes, I've never really done any mountain biking."

"Don't' worry, it's not that hard, and if you do everything I tell you you'll be fine."

"Oh, I love a woman that isn't afraid to take charge," he said jokingly and she responded by smacking him playfully in the arm as he put on his seatbelt and she pulled away.

When they got to the clearing at the base of the mountain Mackenzie parked the car and James helped her take the bikes off the rack on the back of the jeep. She had an extra helmet that she gave him to wear and then she went over some basic safety tips.

"This is a very fun sport, but it is also a dangerous one," she said. She told him that on the way up it wasn't going to be very difficult, but the way down he had to pay attention. She explained that they weren't going to be on a very rough trail, so he just had to stay behind her and do what she does. She explained that he needed to keep his weight to the back of the bike and when he wanted to slow down he should feather the brake. "And most importantly," she said, "as simple as it sounds, you have to remember which lever is for which brake. If anything goes wrong be sure you pull the rear brake first. If you do it the other way around you are going right over your handle bars and you will probably end up getting hurt."

They entered into the woods and started to ride up the mountain. She explained to him how the gears worked and told him that he would have to change them depending on how steep it got and how hard it was for him to peddle the bike. He followed her as she took her time riding up the main trail. When she got to the top she stopped and looked back. He was still a good way down the mountain trying his best to catch up to her. She stood at the top and watched as he lowered the gear and peddled up to her. When he finally got there he stepped down off the peddles and was breathing heavily trying to catch his breath.

"Come on...That was nothing!" she said teasingly.

"I told you I've never done this before," he responded through his pants.

She turned her bike around and faced the back side of the mountain and watched as the sun broke the tops of the trees. "This is what I wanted to show you," she said as she looked out.

"It is beautiful," he said.

"Yes, it is...But that's not why I wanted to show it to you." She saw the puzzled look he gave her from the corner of her eye. She was silent for a while and then looked down the mountain. Unlike the side with the trails, this side was a pretty steep drop with a lot of trees and rocks. She took a deep breath and finally spoke again. "This is where my brother died."

"What?" James asked in a very surprised voice.

"It wasn't very long after we moved here. He found these old trails up here and it became his favorite place in the world. When he wasn't riding them he was working on them. Digging up roots, building jumps, clearing debris...anything to make them better. One day, he just never came home. When he wasn't home by dinner my parents called the police to report him missing. They called all his old friends, looked all over, but they didn't find him. Not until the next day when I thought to come here. One of the state troopers came with me and we found him down there," she said as she pointed to a steep area with a cluster of rocks at the bottom.

"You found him! That had to be horrible."

"It wasn't easy, that's for sure, but the worst part for me is not knowing what happened. The police found no signs of foul play and eventually closed it out as an accident. Some other people became convinced that it was suicide. That wasn't easy either. I just don't know what happened. He was too good of a rider to have an accident like that, and suicide...that just isn't possible. My brother was my best friend. We told each other everything and there is no way he would have killed himself."

"I had no idea."

"I know, not too many people do. Like I said, it wasn't long after we moved here so we didn't really know a lot of people yet."

"How can you come back here like this after everything that has happened?"

"I come here every week. I guess it's kinda like you going to the church. It helps me feel close to him."

"Yeah, but that's only because I am forced to be

here. If it were up to me I would never be in this town again. You know that."

"But that's exactly why I brought you here," she said as she turned to him and took his hands in hers. "What happened to your mother was a tragedy. What happened to my brother was a tragedy. There is no question about either one of those facts, but the way it affected the two of us is very different. You let the death of your mother keep you away from a place you used to love. A place you used to look forward to coming to."

"It was just too hard. I didn't want to remember."

"But you have to remember," she said firmly. "When my brother died I didn't come here for a while, but then I realized that life is a precious thing and now, I live it to the fullest. I come here every week to do just that, as well as to remember my brother's life. I came to accept that he is gone and I will probably never know why, but that doesn't mean I didn't find any answers. I still found answers."

James' eyes perked with intrigue. "What answers?" he asked. "What answers did you find?"

"People come in and out of your life all the time. You have to cherish the time you have with them and grow from each and every experience. When you lose someone that you love, a person that was a big influence in your life, it is certainly hard. But those are defining moments in one's life. You eventually have to decide if you are going to let that awful loss control you, or if you are going to grow from the time you had with that person and live a full, happy life."

Fourteen

Jerry woke up the same time as he did every other day, but because there was no job scheduled they boys took the opportunity to sleep in. He was having his morning coffee and reading the paper when the phone rang. He casually walked to the wall where the phone hung and answered it.

"Hello?"

"Hello," a man replied. "Is this Jerry Collins?"

"Yes, yes it is."

"I have heard very good things about your work and I was hoping you would be available for a job."

"Thank you, I'm sure I could be. What kind of job do you have in mind?" They discussed the specifics and Jerry agreed to meet a half hour later to make an estimate.

Jerry finished his coffee while he brewed another cup into his large travel mug. He threw on a pair of jeans and headed out to his truck. When he got the site of the job his new potential client was there waiting for him in front of the large building. They went inside and again discussed exactly what it was the client wanted done. Jerry agreed and then proceeded to take measurements and write them down into a notebook. He estimated the cost of material and labor and then sat down to discuss a final price.

"All that's left now is the matter of permits," Jerry said.

"Don't worry about any of that," replied the man. "I have taken care of everything. I am getting them from the building inspector tomorrow and I was hoping you could start working Wednesday morning if that works for you."

"That sounds great," Jerry agreed. The men shook hands and then Jerry made his way back to his truck.

On his way back home he stopped to pick up his order of new carpet for the pontoon boat from a local boat shop. By the time he got back to the house the boys were awake and probably wondering where he had been because he left in such a hurry he forgot to leave a note. He went inside and told them he needed a hand in the driveway and when they got outside they saw he had the truck backed up by where the boat was parked.

"How about we get this carpet down?" he said.

"Yes!" Ryan said excitedly.

"Okay then, let's get to work." He said to his kids.

The seats were already removed from when James and Ryan tore up the old carpet and the only thing keeping the deck from being completely empty was the new console that James and Billy had recently installed. James removed the console from the deck and disconnected all the necessary cables. With the deck totally bare they laid out the new carpet and cut it to size. Once everything was ready they pulled back half of the carpet and began to spread the adhesive.

"So, I got a pretty interesting phone call this morning," Jerry said while they were working.

"Yeah, what's that, Dad?" James asked without looking up as he dragged the trowel across the wood of the deck.

"Tom Wilson called and wanted to talk about a job. I ended driving up to the north shore to see him. They want to remodel the HOA's clubhouse and he hired me for the job."

"What kind of remodeling?" Ryan asked.

"Everything," Jerry responded. "They want me to completely gut the interior down to a shell and do an entire rebuild. They are going to change the entire floor plan so I'm going to have to frame out all new rooms. They want a bigger common room for parties, they want to move the gym, and they want the office on the other side of the building. It's going to be a lot of work and it's probably going to take the rest of the summer."

"That really does sound like a lot. Can you handle all that?" James asked.

"Of course, that's nothing compared to the stuff I used to do. This could be a very good thing for me guys. If I do well on this job it could lead to me getting a lot more work. A lot bigger jobs, just like I used to do."

He could hear the excitement in his father's voice and he was happy for him, but he still thought it sounded like a lot of work.

"That's great, Dad, but in the city you had an entire crew of people to help you out. Just make sure you don't take on more than you can handle. If you need any help don't hesitate to ask."

"What was that?" Jerry responded with a sarcastically stunned tone to his voice. "Did I just hear what I think I heard? Did you just offer to help me with a job?"

"Yes, I did. It sounds like a lot of work, and I'm sure I'm going to regret saying this, but I think I might almost be starting to enjoy spending some time with you guys."

"Now there's something I never thought I would hear you say. But seriously, thanks."

"I want to help, too," Ryan added eagerly.

"We can all do it together. It is a big job and I was hoping you guys would help me out."

They finished gluing down the section of carpet they were working on and rolled back the other side to finish the job. Ryan applied the glue and James laid the carpet in place. Once it was down they used rolling pins to press it flat. They ensured that there were no lumpy areas and that they had proper adhesion over the entire deck. They stood back and admired their work. They thought it would take much longer than it actually did, but the way they worked together really showed them that they made a good team. James reconnected all the cables for the console and mounted it back into place. They tested everything to make sure it worked like it was supposed to and they were done. Now, they just needed to get the old seats reupholstered and the boat would be ready to go.

Fifteen

Once they started the new north shore job it seemed like they were all working from sunup to sundown, and it was still only the first week. They were in the demolition phase and everything in the place had to go. Carpets had to be ripped up, hardwood floors removed, and sheetrock and walls had to be knocked down. As fun as it was to destroy things, it was some serious work. At one point on the second day Ryan got a little too ahead of himself. While trying to take down a wall, with maybe a little too much excitement, he ended up busting a water line that he didn't know was there. James had never seen his father change attitudes so quickly before in his life. They all went from joking around and just kind of breaking stuff to their father yelling about not taking the job seriously and rushing through things. It was easy enough to shut the water off, but fixing the pipe definitely set them back by at least half a day. They all took their time a little more since then to avoid any more setbacks.

The work had James so occupied he hadn't been

able to see Mackenzie since the job started, and for that fact alone the weekend couldn't get there soon enough. They were texting throughout the day and he would call her every night, mostly just to hear her voice, but it wasn't enough for either of them. When James would call her after work, all he really wanted to do was eat something and get ready to go to sleep because he knew he had to be up by six o'clock the next morning. He was beat, and he knew that for the most part it was going to be like this for the rest of the summer. It shouldn't take too long for his body to get used to the schedule, and his father said once they reached a good point in the job the hours wouldn't go so late, but right now, it was all but killing him.

Friday finally came and James worked harder than he had all week because he couldn't wait for the day to be over. After recuperating for the night once he got home, he was planning to wake up on Saturday and spend every minute of the weekend with Mackenzie. That was until his father came up to him and Ryan at about seven o'clock that night and told them that they were going to have to work the next day.

"But tomorrow is Saturday," James exclaimed.

"I understand that, son, and I am sorry, but if we want to get ahead of this job and ever have a normal schedule it has to be done. It's only one Saturday."

"But, Dad, I have plans. I know this job is important to you, but I do have a life outside of work."

"I know, and I can't tell you how much I appreciate the sacrifice that you and your brother are making for me and our family. I need you guys here, and I promise it won't be a regular thing."

"Fine, I will push back my plans. But I am going to

hold you to what you just said. As important as this job is, working on Saturdays better not become a norm."

James sent Mackenzie a text telling her that he had to work and wasn't going to be able to see her. She sent a response almost instantly.

No prob. I know how important this job is to ur Dad.

But I want to see you, he wrote back. The abbreviated texts still drove him crazy, but he accepted it from her without argument.

U will, jst not as soon as u hoped.

* * *

They ended work on Saturday earlier than they had the rest of the week. James was still pretty exhausted, but he had planned for Mackenzie to come over and spend the evening at the house. When he got home with his father and brother Mackenzie was already there, and she had brought dinner for them. They were all very surprised by this, but happy because they hadn't planned anything. While they ate everyone was very quiet and it was clear they had all been working very hard. She broke the silence by mentioning that while she was waiting for them she noticed all the work they had done on the new boat and how good it was starting to look.

"It's just about there," James said. "It just needs new seat covers."

"Is that something you can buy?" she asked.

"Well it probably is, but you'll never get a perfect fit that way," Jerry said. "Making your own custom seats is certainly the best way to go."

"That's something Mom would have been able to do," Ryan added.

"Yes, it is," Jerry responded. "And it's something she probably would have really enjoyed."

Mackenzie saw how much they missed her and understood what this boat meant to all of them. She looked at James, who was obviously getting upset by the thought of his mother, and before she knew what she was saying the words were coming out of her mouth.

"Would you mind if made them?" she asked.

"You know how to do that?" James asked her.

"Well, I have never made seat covers before, but I have done my fair share of sewing and I would really like to give it a try, if it's okay with you?"

"I think that is a great idea," Jerry said before giving James a chance to answer.

Mackenzie was happy with his answer, but she still looked at James to see his reaction. Finally, he agreed and she couldn't help but smile. She felt an overwhelming pleasure being accepted into this project that obviously meant so much to all of them.

After dinner they went out to the garage where the seats were and she took all the measurements and drew a quick sketch of the seats so she would have something to work off of. When she was satisfied that she had enough to go with she tucked her notebook into her bag and they headed down to the fire pit by the water. Ryan had already lit the fire and the flames were really starting to grow by the time they had gotten there. They spent the rest of the night talking about possible colors for the seats and ultimately the conversation turned back to their mother. James sat there, holding Mackenzie in his arms at the fireside. There was a mild coolness to the summer air and a light mist over the water which caused Mackenzie to bury herself deeper in the warm embrace of his arms as they reminisced about the memories of their mother.

At the end of the night James walked Mackenzie to her jeep. He kissed her goodnight and hugged her tight against his body. In that moment she felt close to him. She felt closer to him than she had ever felt with anyone else. It was like she was just fully admitted into his world. They had shared so much with each other recently. Things they had both never shared with anyone else, and it felt amazing.

She got into the driver's seat and started the engine. Before she drove away she told him that she had tickets to see a concert the next day and asked him if he would take her.

"Who's playing?" he asked.

"It's an indie band playing down at Bethel Woods. It's going to be a great show."

"I don't know," he said wearily. "Indie's not really my thing."

"Come on. It will be fun. I promise."

He showed a little reluctance but ultimately agreed and gave her one more kiss goodnight.

"Good. Pick me up at six," she said and then drove away.

* * *

The next morning while Mackenzie was at church James took the opportunity to spend the day with Billy. They met in town for some breakfast and then stuck to their normal routine of fishing and simply wasting the day away on the lake.

"So, how are things going with you?" Billy asked.

"Not bad. My father is working us like crazy on this new north shore job, but other than that, everything is pretty good."

"I hear you're almost done with the pontoon boat."

"Yeah, just about, the only thing left is the new seat covers. Mackenzie is going to make them."

"You two have really hit it off, huh? I got to tell you, I never would have seen that happening." Billy said with a slight chuckle.

"Well sometimes these things just happen like that."

"I guess sometimes they do."

James could tell that Billy was finally starting to accept the fact that he was with Mackenzie by the way he hadn't been giving him a hard time over her being a north shore girl anymore. He got the feeling there was more that Billy wanted to say, but he wasn't going to push it. This was one of the few times they discussed his relationship without Billy criticizing everything about it, and he didn't want to start an argument.

As it started to get later James and Billy packed up their gear and headed in off the lake. They were planning on going into town and getting some dinner before James had to pick up Mackenzie for the concert. When they got to Main Street the entire block was taken up with parked cars, so James had to park around the corner from the pizzeria. They were walking up the street when James caught sight of Chad walking towards him. He felt a sense of annoyance wash over him and hoped that there wouldn't be any type of confrontation. It was obvious the only reason Chad ever gave him a hard time was to make him look bad and show off in front of Mackenzie. He quickly knew things weren't going to go that smoothly once they made eye contact and a devious smirk stretched across Chad's face.

As they passed each other Chad threw his shoulder into James. "Why don't you watch where you're going," he yelled as if the whole thing was James' fault.

"Why don't you just back off," James replied.

"Well would you look at that, guys," Chad said as he turned to his two cronies Kurt and Derek. "He walks into me, and rather than apologizing, he snaps at me."

With that they all started to laugh.

"Give me a break," James said.

"Listen here city boy, your girlfriends not here to protect you this time. What do you say we settle this right now?"

"I told you before, Chad, I'm not going to fight you. Not now, not ever." James turned and walked away with Billy and as the entered the pizzeria he heard Chad yell one final thing, but he was unable to make out what it was, and he didn't care enough to go back out and find out.

After dinner James had to go straight to pick up Mackenzie. He was already running a little late, but they still had plenty of time to make it to the concert. Half way to her house his truck wasn't riding right but he tried to ignore it. After driving about another half mile he had to pull over and check it out because there was definitely something wrong. He walked around the truck to find his front passenger side tire completely flat. He went to the back of the truck to pull out his jack and the spare tire and hoped he could change it quickly to get to Mackenzie's. When he slid the jack under the truck he realized the extension arm used to crank it up was broken and wouldn't attach to the jack. "Just great," he said out loud. "That's just my luck." He grabbed a screwdriver from his toolbox and shoved it into the jack where the appropriate tool was supposed to go. He managed to lift the truck off the ground, but without the leverage of the extension arm it took a lot longer than it should have.

Once he got the flat tire off he found a nail in it. "Great, that job hasn't been enough of a pain in my ass, now I'm picking up nails in my tire," he said for no one to hear. He put the spare on and lowered the truck just as slowly as he had jacked it up. He threw everything in the bed of the truck, dusted himself off and took off to Mackenzie's.

When he pulled up in front of her door she immediately came out to him and got in the truck. "Where were you, you were supposed to be here forty-five minutes ago."

"I'm sorry, I got a flat tire. Then, the damn jack was broken and it took forever to get the truck in the air and change it."

"Whatever," she said with an obvious tone of frustration in her voice. "We can't change what time it is now. Let's just get going so we don't miss the show."

They headed out through town again and towards the highway. There was a lot more traffic than James thought there would be. Of course Sunday was a bad day for traveling in the Catskills because everybody was on their way home from their weekend houses, but he figured at almost seven o'clock at night it would have let up.

"We're never going to make it there before the show starts," Mackenzie said.

"We'll make it," James responded, "don't worry."

When the traffic finally started moving James took off like he was in the Indy 500. He weaved between cars pushing the speed of his truck more than he normally would. With only about ten or fifteen minutes left to their trip he hit a bump and instantly felt his rear right tire go flat. He almost lost control of the truck it happened so fast but he safely pulled into the shoulder. He got out to look at it and sure enough it was completely flat. He felt around the tire. "Another nail!" he yelled. "What the hell are the chances of that?"

"What's going on?" Mackenzie asked opening the passenger window.

"I've got another nail in the tire. The bump must have been too much for it."

"So now what?"

"I don't have another spare. We're going to have to wait for a tow truck."

It took the tow truck over an hour to get there, and by the time they got to the garage and got the tire fixed it was after nine o'clock.

"The concert is at least a half an hour away," James said when they got back in the truck. "What do you want to do?"

"By the time we get there it will be almost over, it's pointless to even go in that direction," Mackenzie snapped. "Just take me home."

Sixteen

"I am so sick of this guy!" Chad yelled in frustration to his friends Derek and Kurt. "What else do I have to do to break these two up?"

They were sitting in Chad's house. Well, the guest house behind his parent's house that he had claimed as his own a year prior.

"Well maybe tonight did the trick." Derek said.

"Yeah, there's no way those old tires held up after you put the nails in them." Kurt said laughing.

"Well, I guess we will see. But I'm not going to be satisfied until that prick is gone and Mackenzie realizes she is supposed to be with me. I don't know what else I can do. Things were fine before he came along. The way it was going it was only a matter of time before she realized how much we belong together."

"Don't worry, Chad," Derek said. "She will come around. You two are perfect for each other. How much can she really have in common with this guy? He is just a summer fling. Once the new toy thing gets old she'll be back."

Kurt sat off to the side a little confused. "Weren't you guys only together for a little while before she broke up with you?"

"Shut up you idiot!" Chad snapped at him. "First of all, she didn't break up with me. We just kind of stopped seeing each other. And secondly, how many people did she date after that? None. We never stopped hanging out. I guess she just wasn't ready for that kind of relationship yet. Then, just as she was starting to come around, this guy shows up and manipulates her into thinking he's something he's not."

"So what are you going to do?" Kurt asked.

"Things are already in the works. I pointed him and his family out to her father at the Fourth of July parade and he didn't seem very happy to see who his daughter was spending all her time with. Between that and his recent car troubles ruining their date, it won't be long before she is back in my arms."

"You sure that's going to work?" Kurt asked.

"You really are a moron aren't you? Of course it's going to work. What can that guy really have to offer her? She will see soon that he might be fun to spend a summer with, but me...I can offer her a future. I can offer her security. How do you think that guy will take care of her? I'm going to an Ivy League school. After that I'll go to law school, and when I'm finished, I'll make more in a year than that guy will in five."

"You're absolutely right," Derek chimed in. "There is no way a guy like him will ever be able to support the lifestyle that she is used to. She needs a guy like you. She'll figure that out soon enough."

"I just want that guy out of the picture," Chad said again. "The end of the summer can't come soon enough.

The faster that guy gets out of town the better."

Seventeen

It took a few days for Mackenzie to get over missing the concert. James knew that she didn't really blame him. It's not like he could control getting the flat tires, but she was pretty upset. He convinced her to let him make it up to her. He refused to tell her what he had planned, but he was confident it was something she would really enjoy. He worked the same long hours they had been doing for the rest of that week and by the time the weekend came Mackenzie was practically torturing him to find out where he was taking her. He stayed strong, knowing it would ruin the surprise if he told her, and that just made her all the more curious.

He picked her up from her house Saturday morning at around nine o'clock. She climbed in the truck and they headed out for the highway.

"So where exactly are you taking me on this mysterious date?"

"No, no. I've held out this long without telling you, I'm not about to spoil everything now. You are just going to have to be patient and find out when we get there."

"Come on," she says as she slides closer to him. "That's not fair. I promise I'll be just as surprised if you tell me now."

"That's not going to happen. This took a lot of planning and I want to make sure everything is perfect."

"I'm sure it will be, but it would be a lot better if I at least had an idea of what we were doing."

"Just trust me. I think it is something you are really going to love."

After driving down Route 17 for almost an hour and a half they reached the New York State Thruway where James continued to drive south.

"This is crazy," Mackenzie said. "We have been driving forever, how much longer until we get to this 'secret location'?"

"Probably about another hour, maybe a little more depending on traffic."

"This is quite a hike. I sure hope whatever it is you planned is worth it," she said in a sarcastic tone of voice.

"Nice try, but I'm still not telling you where we are going. It will be worth it, and I can guarantee you are going to have a good time."

A little while later they crossed the Tappan Zee Bridge and Mackenzie started to see signs for New York City. She started to grow a bit excited and asked him more questions about what they were doing. The way she eagerly asked if they were going to the city reminded him of the excitement in a child when opening birthday presents. She was very obviously filled with wonder and anticipation. He could see in her face that she wanted to know now more than ever exactly what he had planned.

As he turned off the Bronx River Parkway he drove into the neighborhood he knew better than anywhere else in the world. He reminisced as he drove down the streets making his way towards his old block. Eventually, he turned onto a side street and pulled over.

"You see that house there?" he asked, then, without waiting for a response he continued to speak. "That's the house I grew up in."

"It's cute," she said. "Looks like a nice place. Where exactly are we?"

"Morris Park, the Bronx. I miss this place. Nowhere else has really felt like home since I left here."

"Home is more than just a house," she said. "It is where you feel comfortable. A place where no matter what is happening in your life, you can go there and feel a sense of ease. The way you described your family's house on the lake to me makes me believe you used to feel at home there. You just have to allow that feeling to come back."

"You are a very intelligent person, you know that? To be honest with you, I think it has a little. Not right away, but as time has gone by, and with the help of some of the new people in my life, I have learned to feel more at home there."

She looked into his eyes and kissed him. It was a deep, passionate kiss that warmed her entire body instantly. As she pulled away she felt a quick chill shoot up her spine when her lips separated from his. She knew that she had fallen for him, fast and hard. This has been the best summer of her life, and although she was pretty sure he felt the same way, they never actually talked about their feelings for each other.

"So, what else do you have planned for today? You

didn't bring me all the way down here to just show me your old house, did you?"

"No, I didn't."

They drove down the block to a deli where they each ordered a sandwich. Once they got everything they needed for lunch they climbed back into the truck and started to drive again. They only went a couple of blocks to a large park. James found a place to park and then grabbed a blanket from the bed of the truck. The park was made up of a playground at both ends, a baseball field in the middle and off to one side was a handball court. In between all this there were plenty of grassy clearings where children were running and playing. Mackenzie followed him as he led her to an open spot in the back of the park under the shade of some of trees. He laid out the blanket and they sat down next to each other.

"When I was a kid we used to come here every weekend. We would always set up a blanket in this spot and eat lunch. When we were finished my brother and I would run around and spend the rest of the day play-ing."

"Sounds like a pretty nice way to spend the day."

"It was, but as we got older my brother and I didn't want to spend every weekend with the family so by the time I was thirteen that all stopped."

They ate their lunch and watched as the young chil-dren ran around. Some were flying kites, others seemed to be playing tag, and another group was kicking around a soccer ball that found its way onto their blan-ket more than once. The older kids were mostly hanging out at the handball court, and based on the cheering and yelling coming from there it seemed like they had some type of a tournament going on.

By the time they finished eating, talking, and watching everybody enjoy their day about two hours had gone by. They cleaned up after themselves and James folded up their blanket. They walked back to the truck and James tossed the blanket in the bed. Then, he reached out for her hand and kept walking. She was a little confused when they didn't get back in the truck and realized he must have more planned. They walked down the sidewalk along the park until they reached an intersection. They turned left and continued walking around the outside of the park. They walked through a tunnel that brought them under some highway and when they came out the other side she saw a huge fence with large letters spelling out BRONX ZOO.

"The Bronx Zoo! We're going to the Bronx Zoo? I've never been here before."

"It really is a remarkable place. I worked here one summer when I was a kid. It's very big, but I'll give you the best tour of it you could ever get."

They spent hours walking around the zoo seeing all the different animals. At some of the exhibits James would stop and tell her a little bit about the animals, a lot of it she knew already, or she could have read it off the sign for herself, but she enjoyed listening to him tell her about them.

"Oh look, over there, it's the monkey cage. I love the monkeys. Let's go see them." Before James even had a chance to answer her she took him by the hand and was dragging him behind her as she hurried to the exhibit. "Look how cute they are."

"Well actually," James said, "these are apes, not monkeys. They are called gibbons and they happen to be my favorite. I actually spent a lot of time over here that summer I worked here."

"Really? So what can you tell me about them?"

"Well I know a lot about them, but if you want to get real specific I'll tell you about one in particular."

"Just one? What could you tell me about just one of them that is different than all the rest?"

"Let's talk about that one over there," James said as he pointed to the back corner. "That is Clevis and he has a pretty fascinating story."

"How could you possibly tell one from another? It's been years since you worked here."

"True, but like I said, there is a story behind Clevis. It is both beautiful and sad at the same time. And I can tell him apart from all the others because of that mark he has on his right leg."

"Okay, tell me this story."

"Well, you see how he is the only one just sitting there while all the others are jumping around or climbing on stuff?"

"Yeah, he almost looks sad."

"Well he wasn't always like that. When I first got a job here he was just like every other gibbon, but before that summer was over that all changed. First let me tell you a little bit about gibbons. They are mostly found in tropical and subtropical rainforests. Each gibbon has their own song. It's actually said that their songs have a type of regional accent based on where they live, just like how we have accents. This song is used to establish their territory, but also, to attract a mate."

"So it's kind of like a love song?" Mackenzie interrupted.

"Well, yeah, you could call it that. Now once they

find that mate, unlike any other apes, they mate for life. Now from what I am told, when Clevis was brought here he was brought with his mate. Her name was Trudy. While I was working here Trudy got some kind of infection. It was pretty serious and while she was sick all Clevis did was pace around that corner like he was nervously waiting for her to come back. Then, one day she just died. That same day he stopped pacing and just sat down, almost as if he knew what had happened. He didn't eat for days after that and the vets were afraid he slipped into some type of depression.

"After that summer I stopped by here every once in a while just to see him and he still sat right there in that corner. Now, four years later, he's still sitting there. It is terribly sad and terribly romantic at the same time."

"That poor thing," Mackenzie said. "Could you imagine completely living to be with that one mate and then all of a sudden they are gone and you just don't know how to go on without them?"

James turned and looked into her eyes and said, "No, no I couldn't."

In that moment Mackenzie knew that James felt the same way about her as she did about him. There was no denying it. She loved him and she knew that he loved her.

James looked at his watch and jumped slightly. "That is going to have to be the end of our tour for today, if we don't leave now we are going to miss our dinner plans."

* * *

When they pulled up in front of a church Mackenzie was a little confused. She looked around and didn't see a single restaurant on the street. "I thought you said we were going to dinner?" she asked.

"We are, come on."

They walked around to the side of the church and down a flight of stairs into the basement. When they walked in the large room was filled with rows of tables much like the cafeteria of a high school. She saw all sorts of people from men, to women, to entire families sitting at the tables eating. Around them stood many more people on a line that wrapped around the entire room still waiting to be served. She followed James, who walked through the room like he knew exactly where he was going. He went to the kitchen and asked for Carol.

"Are you my new two?" a woman yelled from behind them.

"Yes," James said turning around and introducing himself and Mackenzie. "What can we do to help?"

"Grab a couple aprons off the wall and go work the counter. Stacey and Jeff could use some help serving."

"No problem," James said as he nodded to Mackenzie and they headed off to do as they were told.

"And hey," Carol yelled to them while she was in the processes of walking away. "Thanks for helping out."

They spent the next couple of hours serving whatever food came out of the kitchen. While they worked they spoke to the regular staff as well as to the people on the other side of the counter. When things slowed down James and Mackenzie walked around the dining area to check on people and see if there was anything else they needed. Mackenzie occasionally sat down with some of the people and just listened as they told their stories of how they ended up there. One man told her about the wonderful life he had before, but after he got addicted to drugs it all slipped away from him.

"Not all at once, of course, but little by little," he said. "Before I knew it, it was too late. The drugs became the most important thing to me and I lost everything because of it. My family. My home. Everything."

Another man told her his story. He told her about how before he ended up where he is now he had a job, went to church every Sunday, and coached his son's little league baseball team. He lost his job because of a company downsizing and couldn't find another. After a while he started taking any work he could get, but it just wasn't enough. They ended up selling their home and moving their family of four into a small one bedroom apartment. They still did the best they could, but sometimes they just didn't have enough money left over to buy food.

She was touched by what she had experienced that night in a way she never thought possible. She couldn't stop talking about it the entire way home. When they got back to her house she took off her seatbelt and turned towards James.

"I had the most amazing time today," she said. "Thank you so much."

"I'm glad you enjoyed it. It really meant a lot to me, too."

"Listen," she said. "There is something I want to ask you, well, it's something that my parents wanted. They want to meet you. Come over for dinner tomorrow?"

"Sure, I'll be there."

She leaned in and kissed him. She again felt the warmth of his lips course through her. She pulled back slowly and in a little less than a whisper said, "I love you." When she realized what she said she turned away and climbed out of the truck before he had a chance to respond. She ran towards the house and before going through the door yelled back, "Tomorrow night, be here at five thirty."

* * *

As he drove away he was stunned by what she had said. He knew that he was falling for her, and of course the thought of love may have crossed his mind, but she had said it. If she had given him a chance he probably would have said it back, but she ran off so quickly he didn't have any time to react.

Only a couple houses down the road from Mackenzie's house a car suddenly pulled out in front of his truck causing him to swerve off the road and come screeching to a stop. While trying to comprehend what had just happened Chad charged his driver's side door yelling something he couldn't quite make out. Once at his window Chad continued, but now his words were clearer.

"When are you going to get the point? Stay away from her!" he yelled.

"What are you talking about?" James responded. "Mind your own business. Us seeing each other has nothing to do with you."

"It has everything to do with me, and she is my business."

"No she's not, I'm pretty sure she has made that clear."

"Why don't you just give it up? It's never going to work between you two. I have done everything I can think of to keep you apart, but no, you just don't get it."

"What are you talking about?"

"What am I talking about?" Chad repeated. "I've tried to make you look bad, I've tried to fight you, but no, you won't budge. I told her father all about you at the parade. I told him how you are going to ruin his daughter and apparently that did nothing. Then there were the tires. I could have sworn that would have worked, but somehow you still got her to see you again. I just don't get it."

"Wait a minute. You put those nails in my tires?"

"Yeah, but it did nothing. Tell you what, that great job your father has at the North Shore HOA, you want him to keep that contract?"

"Get lost. You have no power over my relationship with Mackenzie, and you certainly have no power over the jobs my father works."

"I may not, but with my father being the president of North Shore HOA, he does."

"And I'm sure he'll let you tell him who to hire and who to fire."

"Hey, if you want to test me, that's your choice. Why don't you just give it up? It's not like this thing with you two is real. She's going to be gone soon anyway."

With that James sat there looking at Chad with a face that must have shown a mixture of annoyance and confusion.

"You don't know, do you?"

"Know what? What the hell are you talking about now?"

"She's leaving the country in a couple weeks. Some mission with the church or something. See, the fact that she didn't tell you just proves that this thing between you isn't real. You're nothing more than a fling. Give it up." Chad stopped talking after that and just walked away laughing to himself.

Eighteen

James didn't want to let Chad get to him. He wanted to believe the things he said were all lies. After all, he had been trying to break them up since before they even really started seeing each other, but in the back of his mind he was still very confused. Granted the summer was ultimately going to come to an end and he was going to have to go back to school, but if she were really leaving the country why wouldn't she have mentioned something about it by now? Why would she wait until the last minute to bring something like that up?

He pulled up to her house at five fifteen. Earlier is always better than later in his opinion, especially if Chad really had been trying to discredit him to her father. When he walked to the door, his entire body was tense with nerves. Of course he had met girl's parents before, but none in a situation as intimidating as this. Just from the outside he could see that his house on the lake would fit in about half of the downstairs of hers. *What if what Chad said is true?* he thought to himself. *What if they already have some preconceived notion that I am no good for their daughter?*

He stood there for a minute hoping that he had dressed properly enough for the evening. He hoped that he wouldn't make some error in table edict that would show him to be uncouth. Fear after fear went through his mind until he finally shook it off and rang the bell. Almost instantly Mackenzie opened the door and greeted him with a kiss. In that moment all his worries faded from his mind and he was reminded that no matter what, she would be there with him and he would be able to overcome any situation.

She led him into the living room where her father was sitting in a chair reading the newspaper. "Dad, this is James. James, this is my father."

Her father set down the newspaper and stood up. He reached out and shook James' hand. "Well, it is nice to finally meet the young man that has been monopolizing all my daughters time," he said before letting loose his grip.

"Well, sir, I very much enjoy her company," James said in response.

"Have a seat son, tell me a little bit about yourself," he said as he sat back down into his chair.

James did as invited and sat on the couch. Mackenzie took the seat right next to him and he felt her slide close to him and take his hand into hers. As long as she was there with him he felt he could handle whatever questions were to come.

"So, James, where do you go to school?" her father asked.

"I just finished my sophomore year at Boston College, sir."

"Boston, that's a very good school. What do you

study?"

"I'm a philosophy major."

"Philosophy, huh? That is an interesting field. What do you hope to do with that when you graduate?"

His nerves instantly came back with that question. "To be honest, Mr. Green, I don't really know. It is just what I enjoy. It is something I believe myself to be good at. To look at the unanswerable questions and try to answer them, it intrigues me."

"So you don't think about the future? About what you want to do after school?"

There it was. The question he had avoided even asking himself. He thought of the best answer he could on the spot. "Well, I would like to continue learning. If all goes well I will probably go to graduate school and continue looking for whatever answers I can along the way. Life is filled with unanswerable questions, what better questions are there than that?"

Just then Mrs. Green came out of the kitchen. "You must be James," she said, breaking the conversation with her husband that James sensed wasn't going very well. "We have heard a lot about you. It is nice to finally meet you."

"Yes, ma'am, thank you for inviting me."

"Oh no, none of that ma'am stuff, and don't even think about calling me Mrs. Green. You can call me Martha."

"Yes, ma'am – ah – Martha."

"Well everybody come on into the dining room, dinner is just about ready."

They walked to a long table where Mackenzie's father took his seat at the head. James sat on the side of the table to his left and Mackenzie next to him. Martha sat to Mr. Green's right across from them, and even though they were all relatively close to one another, the large table still felt rather abandoned. They made small talk for a few more minutes before Martha excused herself and then moments later returned to the table with a large tray of chicken francese.

Dinner went by with very little conversation making it feel as if it took hours. James knew Mr. Green was watching him. Probably critiquing every move he made. He felt very uncomfortable the entire time until, finally, just as everyone was about done eating, Mr. Green broke the deafening silence.

"You don't talk much, do you, son?"

"I'm sorry, sir, to be honest I am just a little nervous."

"Nervous, what could you possibly have to be nervous about?"

"I don't know, sir. Nothing I guess."

"In my experience someone is only nervous if they have something to hide. Is that it young man? Do you have something to hide?"

"Daddy!" Mackenzie interjected.

"It's a simple question," he responded to his daughter before turning back to James.

"No, that's not it at all," James said firmly in an attempt to convince him it was the truth.

"Well then, I don't see why you have any reason not to be yourself."

James knew why he was so nervous. It was because of Chad. Because of everything he had said about it never working out between him and Mackenzie. About how he told her father all about him before they got the chance to meet. He couldn't tell Mr. Green that he was worried about not meeting his approval based on that. He could see where this was going, and it wasn't good. If he admitted that Chad got the better of him it would most likely verify everything that was said about him, so, he simply didn't respond.

Martha began to clear the table and James went back into the living room with Mackenzie and her father. They spoke some more about where James was from and how long his family had a house on the lake. Eventually, the conversation turned back to the future. More specifically it turned to the topic of James' future. James still had no idea what he wanted to do for a living and he could only avoid the topic so much before Mr. Green grew obviously frustrated.

"So, James, you still have not answered my question from earlier. You said you want to further your education by attending graduate school, but you didn't say exactly what it is you want to do when you are done with that."

It was obvious to James that this was where Mr. Green was going to focus most of his attention. That if he kept avoiding the question it would only keep coming back up. He decided to just answer it as honestly as he could. "To be entirely honest with you, sir, I don't really know what I want to do with the rest of my life. I wish I could give you a more specific answer, but I just haven't figured it all out yet."

With that, Mr. Green gave a bit of a disapproving chuckle, got up from his seat and walked out of the room. Mackenzie followed her father down the hall leaving James in the living room just as Martha came in with a fresh pot of coffee and sat down. She could tell something was wrong as she nervously sipped her tea and then asked James if he would like a cup of coffee. He accepted one and just as he took his first sip they began to hear the yelling come from the back room.

"And that's why you're doing all this now isn't it, to get back at me?"

It was Mr. Green yelling at Mackenzie, and although James and Martha weren't able to hear the beginning of the argument James was pretty sure it had something to do with him.

"Not everything has to do with you, Daddy. I can make my own decisions."

"Apparently not very good ones. After everything I did to ensure you got in, you blow off your acceptance to Princeton and tell us that instead of going to college you're going to be running off to some other country with the church. Now, you waste your entire summer with this – this, lost cause."

"So that's what this is all about? It all comes down to Princeton."

"We're Green's, we go to Princeton. Your grandfather went there, your mother and I both went there, your brother was going to go there, and you are going to go there."

"I'm not going to Princeton, Dad. I am my own person and I can make my own choices."

"Yeah, like the great one that is sitting in the living room right now. That boy has no future, he said as much himself."

That was more than James had to hear. It was obvious that he was not welcome by Mackenzie's father and that everything Chad had said was true. Mackenzie was leaving and she didn't even find it important enough to tell him about it. He didn't need to sit around and listen to any more of what was being said.

"I think I should probably go now," James said to Martha as he set his coffee mug down on the table.

"Oh, James, I'm sorry," she replied. "What he's saying really has nothing to do with you."

He painfully forced half a smile across his face and walked out the door.

Nineteen

It had been two weeks since James walked out of Mackenzie's house. It didn't take her long to realize he left that night. Maybe her mother told her he walked out the door, or maybe she heard him start his truck in the driveway, but one way or another she knew and by the time he was pulling out into the street his phone was ringing. He didn't have to look at the caller ID to know it was her, but he didn't answer. Why would he answer? Everything Chad had said was true. She didn't care about him. She was leaving soon to some foreign country and didn't even find it important enough to tell him. How is that evidence of caring. No, he came to realize that he was just one last summer fling. One last carefree moment before she moved on with her life. Well that wasn't good enough for him. He didn't know what he was expecting from their relationship, but it was more than that.

In order to keep his mind occupied he spent his days working with Ryan and his father. He was putting in long hours, and unlike before he didn't complain about it at all. After work he would spend the evenings by himself, usually reading a book down on the dock or fishing until it got so dark he couldn't see his line. He went to sleep early every night and he did everything he could think of to avoid any thoughts of Mackenzie. That wasn't as easy as he thought it would be. It seemed like everything reminded him of her and he realized all he could do was count down the time until he could get back to Boston and hopefully forget about the entire summer.

Every morning for the past couple weeks James woke up early and walked into the kitchen. Every morning his father was already there, sitting at the table drinking his coffee and reading the newspaper. This particular day was no different.

"Good morning, Jim."

"If you say so," James responded with no patience for pleasantries.

Jerry would have been taken back, but this is how the day seemed to start almost every morning recently.

"Coffee's on the counter. And when you're done there is a package on the porch for you."

"For me, I didn't order anything."

Jerry didn't respond so James made his cup of coffee and then walked to the door. When he opened it he found a box there with no delivery label, no return address, and no postage. He curiously brought it inside and pulled the top open. Once he saw the contents he stopped and just stared at it. Inside the box, neatly folded, were the new seat covers for the pontoon boat that Mackenzie had made. He had forgotten all about them, and now, here they were. Without a word James just set the box down on the floor, sat down at the table, and continued to drink his coffee.

Jerry was concerned about the way James had been acting lately, and he knew something was wrong, but he also knew better than to pry. James would talk to him when he was ready. If he was ready. Until then, there wasn't much more he could do for his son.

Ryan came into the room a short time later and saw the box sitting on the floor with the flaps open. He peered in and saw what it was. "Is that what I think it is?" he asked excitedly.

James didn't move. He didn't look up. He didn't say a word. He simply stared into his black coffee as if he didn't hear his brother.

"Come on, what are we waiting for? Let's put them on."

"I don't think that's a very good idea right now," Jerry said.

"Why not, what are you talking about? Come on… James, let's go."

"Ryan," Jerry snapped. "Go get your stuff and head out to the truck. I want to get an early start today. I'll be there in a minute."

Once Ryan was out of the room Jerry turned to James. "Look, I don't know what is going on, but why don't you take the day off. Try to relax a little and work out whatever it is that's bothering you."

"No, I'm good."

"You don't get what I'm saying, James. Take the day off. I don't care what you do, but I don't want you at the jobsite. You need to take some time for yourself."

"Come on, Dad. I'd really rather keep myself busy."

"I know, but something is bothering you and you need to deal with it, not ignore it."

James stormed out of the kitchen and Jerry wanted to follow him, but he knew that unless James came to him to talk it would do no good. He poured the rest of his coffee into his travel mug and headed out to the truck.

"Where's James?" Ryan asked.

"It's just us today, let's go."

* * *

Mackenzie sat alone in her room for a week after that night. She didn't talk to any of her friends, she didn't sit with her parents for meals, and she absolutely avoided any and all contact with her father. He always put so much emphasis on who they were and who she was expected to be because of their last name and she was sick of it. It always drove her crazy, but it was never anything more than annoying. Now it has directly impacted her life. Her father and his ideas of superiority drove away the best guy she had ever known. The guy she had fallen in love with, and now, he won't even answer her calls. In the week she kept herself locked in her room she called and sent more text messages than she could count, all with no reply.

After the first week Mackenzie would only talk to Julie about what had happened. Julie tried to tell her she couldn't just sit around, but it took her almost another week before she talked her into getting out of the house. Once they started going out Julie noticed a change in her best friend. She wasn't the same free spirit anymore. If you could count on Mackenzie for anything it was always seeing the bright side of any situation. It was the way she always made the best out of everything. Now, she seemed like an entirely different person.

"What can I do to help you?" Julie asked her.

"Nothing, there's nothing anyone can do."

"You can't just sulk forever, Kenz. You need to move on. I'm sorry things didn't work out for you, but it's not the end of the world."

"I know that, but I'm sure things could have worked out. Things were going so good between us." She paused for a moment as if to consider what she was about to say next. "Did you know the night before everything happened I told him I loved him? I've never said that to anyone."

"Oh, Mackenzie," she said in the most sympathetic tone. "What did he say?"

"Nothing – He didn't say anything. I didn't give him the chance to. As soon as I said it I couldn't believe the words came out of my mouth. I got so embarrassed I ran out of his truck before he had the chance to say a word. The next day he came over for dinner and thanks to my father and his godforsaken '*We are Green's*' speech I'll never know how he felt."

Twenty

James was sitting home, just as he had been doing every day for almost a week now that his father wouldn't let him work, and he was still trying to find an adequate distraction. Something… Anything he could do that would keep his mind off of Mackenzie. It's been almost three weeks since he'd seen her last and he only missed her more. People always said time was supposed to heal all things. At least, that's what he thought the saying was. Maybe he had it wrong, or maybe it just didn't apply to this situation. Maybe his feelings for Mackenzie were stronger than that. Stronger than any simple proverbial reason.

While he sat quietly trying to figure out how he was going to get over her the doorbell rang. Not expecting any visitors he was a little hesitant to blindly open the door. He went to the living room window and peeked through the curtain to see Billy standing there looking around. *Go away!* James thought to himself as he ducked out of the window, *just go away*. The doorbell rang again and after some hesitation he slowly walked to the door, dragging his feet the entire way hoping Billy would leave before he got there.

"What do you want?" he said monotonically when he opened the door.

"What kind of way is that to greet your buddy? I haven't seen you in a while. You haven't answered your phone, you don't text back... Where have you been, is everything okay with you man?"

"I've been right here, and I'm fine."

"You look like hell. Get dressed, we're going out."

"Not today, Bill. I'm really not feeling up to it."

"Why not? What's up with you man?"

"I'm just not in the mood. Leave it alone."

Billy could clearly see something was bothering James, and unlike his father, Billy wasn't about to let it go. "Listen man, something is obviously bothering you. I'm not leaving here until you tell me about it." Pushing past James Billy walked into the house and disappeared into the kitchen. A moment later he came back with two cups of coffee, James was still standing at the open door when his friend sat down on the couch and set the mugs on the coffee table. "Come on, sit down."

James closed the door and sat across from his friend.

"Now, what's going on?" Billy asked again.

"It's really a pretty long, complicated story."

"Well, I've got all day."

"I don't even know where to start," James said as he picked up his cup.

"How about the beginning," Billy responded as he sat back.

James began to talk. The words seemed to come out fluently, as if he didn't even have to think about what to say, and he told Billy everything. He started with the day in the city and about how she told him that she loved him. He continued on and told him about how Chad stopped him on his way home and tried to fill his head with a bunch of stuff about her. About her not really being interested in him. About how it would never work out between them. About the fact that she was leaving the country at the end of the summer and didn't even tell him.

"You don't really believe all that crap, do you? I mean, look at the source. It's Chad. You know he would say anything to break you two up."

"That's what I thought," James said. "And I'm pretty sure he could tell I wasn't buying it. But there's more..." James told Billy about the threat Chad made about having his father's contract with the North Shore HOA pulled. "That shook me a little bit, and he could tell. That job is everything to my father right now. I can't let him lose it because of me."

"So you aren't seeing her because of that?"

"I wish that were it, Billy. I really do." He went on to tell him about the next night. How he showed up for dinner and did everything he could to be perfect, but no matter what, it just didn't seem to be good enough. He told him about how it seemed like everything he said was wrong. How it was obvious that her father didn't like him. Then, he told him about the argument Mackenzie had with her father after dinner. About how he heard every word they said and he obviously wasn't welcome there. Wasn't good enough to associate with her nevertheless date her. He told him that as their argument continued the things they were yelling about confirmed everything Chad had said. She was leaving, and soon.

It took everything for James not to completely break down in front of his friend.

"Did you talk to her about it?" Billy asked.

"No, why would I do that? I heard everything I needed to hear."

"So what did you do?"

"What do you think I did? I left. I just got up and walked out."

"Just like that? You just left and didn't even give her a chance to explain?"

"Explain what? Everything Chad said was true. I don't need to hear it all over again from her."

"Man. That really sucks. I'm sorry."

"Yeah, me too."

They sat quietly for a while and then again Billy told James to get up and get dressed.

"For what?"

"I already told you, we are going out. Now I think you need it even more than I did before."

"I really don't feel like it. I'm just going to stay home."

"No way, I think you have probably stayed home enough. You need to get out. You'll never be able to get all of this stuff out of your mind if you are sitting here alone."

"Fine," James finally agreed. "But don't expect me to be too entertaining."

* * *

Julie was happy to see that Mackenzie was finally starting to get back into a routine. This Saturday was no different from any other and Mackenzie had to set up the classroom at the church for their Sunday class. Since she stopped seeing James, Julie had been picking her up and helping with the prep work so they could spend more time together. Mackenzie was starting to act a little more like herself, but Julie was pretty sure that she was just covering up her pain. She knew how much James meant to her, and the way they split up was not something anyone could easily get over.

When they got into town they decided to get some breakfast at the diner before heading to the classroom. While they were eating someone interrupted their conversation.

"Well hey there. Where have you been hiding?"

Mackenzie looked up to see Chad standing next to the table looking down at her.

"I haven't been hiding!" she said in a tone that came off as very defensive.

"Hey now, it's just an expression. I didn't mean anything by it."

"I'm sorry, I didn't mean to snap. How have you been?"

"I'm good. How about you? It's been a while."

"I've been better," she said while looking away from the conversation.

"What's wrong? You don't seem like your usual upbeat self."

"It's nothing. I don't really want to talk about it."

"Alright," Chad said. "Do you mind if I join you guys for a cup of coffee?"

Mackenzie shot a look, which was really more of a glare, at Julie when she heard her say, "Of course, grab a seat."

Chad looked at Julie, then back at Mackenzie and

said, "Good, I've missed hanging out with you guys," and sat down next to Mackenzie.

They sat making small talk while they ate their food and the waitress brought Chad a cup of coffee.

"So where have you been, Mackenzie?" Chad asked.

"I've been around. It's been a pretty busy summer."

There was an awkward silence after that for a few moments until Chad finally asked, "So how are things with you and your boyfriend?"

Julie stopped chewing her food and just looked at him. He noticed the instant reaction and looked back at Mackenzie who was just looking down at her plate, pushing some eggs around with her fork. After a long moment of no one speaking Mackenzie said, without looking up, "We're not really seeing each other any-more."

"Oh, I'm sorry, I didn't know. Are you okay? What happened?" Chad said with the most sincere, concerned voice.

"I really don't want to get into it," she said, still refusing to look up and obviously trying not to let her emotions show. "It just didn't work out."

"That's too bad," Chad said as he slid a little closer to her and put his hand on her shoulder. "If you ever need to talk you know I'm here for you. I always have been, and nothing will ever change that."

"Yeah, I know. Thanks, but I'll be fine."

Again silence came over the table. It was obvious that there was more than what was being said and no one knew how to properly change the subject. Chad didn't let on that he knew anything and was hoping that

James hadn't mentioned to Mackenzie his part in the situation, but just by her allowing him to sit down he was pretty sure that she didn't know anything. Just as he was trying to figure out what to say next Julie's phone rang.

"Ugh, it's my mother," she said. Julie always hated when her parents interrupted her while she was out. "Hello?"

"What do you mean? What happened?"

Mackenzie and Chad could see the look of immediate concern sweep over her face as they listened to her side of the conversation.

"Why won't you just tell me what's going on?"

"Fine," she finally said argumentatively. "I'll be right there."

As she hung up the phone Mackenzie and Chad just looked at her to see if she would tell them what was going on. When she didn't, Mackenzie asked her if everything was okay.

"I have no idea. She said I have to come home right away. Do you mind if I bring you home?"

"You don't have to do that," Chad said. I'll make sure she gets home. Go make sure everything is okay."

Julie turned to Mackenzie. "Do you mind?"

"Of course not… Go. I'll take care of the classroom and then go with Chad. I hope everything is alright."

"Thank you," Julie said and then she grabbed her stuff and headed out the door.

After Julie left the waitress brought the bill to the table. Before Mackenzie could pick it up Chad grabbed it and headed to the cashier.

"You didn't have to do that," she said when she caught up to him at the door.

"I know, but I wanted to. It's not often we spend time together, just consider it my way of saying it's nice to hang out with you again."

"Well, thank you."

"Don't mention it."

* * *

Billy brought James to an empty field that had been turned into a driving range before either of them even knew what golf was. Golf was not something that James made a habit of playing when he lived in The Bronx, but when he was in Roscoe it was always a good way to spend time. James and Billy would spend hours hitting balls at the driving range. Making bets with each other on who could hit the ball farther, who had better accuracy, or who had a better swing. Roscoe also had a small nine hole golf course that they would play every once in a while, but James hadn't been there in years. As a matter of fact, James hadn't touched a golf club since the last time he was there with Billy.

After a little while of just smashing the ball as hard as he could, James started to feel himself calm down and he was able to focus on his form. He began hitting the ball as well as he used to and he remembered why he enjoyed golf. It wasn't a fast game, and he never really considered it much of a sport, but he enjoyed it because it always helped him clear his mind. When he slowed down and focused on what he was doing, it was hard to think about anything else. He didn't want to admit it at first, but being there with Billy was actually helping.

Eventually they started to critique each other's swings the way they used to. Then, they had a few contests to see who could hit the ball farther. Billy won most of them, not to any surprise of James seeing how he was so out of practice. But eventually the topic of Mackenzie came up again.

"So, she's really leaving?" Billy asked.

"Yeah, she is."

"When? Where is she going?"

"I don't have the slightest idea."

"When do you go back to school?"

"Two weeks."

"You know what I think?" Billy said. "I think that you knew you were going to have to leave anyway. It's a fact that I'm sure you were avoiding all summer with her. Even before you knew she was leaving, you knew you were. Now, this is just an easy way for you to do it. Blame her father for the things he said. Blame her for not telling you she was leaving. Blame anyone you can to make going back to school easier. But it's not making it any easier is it? You miss her, and if you don't set things straight with her it's going to haunt you."

"When did you get so deep? I thought you were the one that tried to keep me from going out with her in the first place."

"Yeah, I was. Then I saw what you two had. Tell me one thing, and if you don't answer me the way I think you will I will drop the whole thing and never mention it again."

"Now that's a deal I'll agree to. What do you want to know?"

"Do you love her?"

James went silent. He looked down at his feet and buried the head of his golf club into the dirt. He pulled it out and wiped it off with his foot, then lifted his head and looked Billy straight in the eyes. "Yeah, I do... I really do."

"Then you need to call her. You have to set everything straight and tell her how you feel. Whatever happens after that is up to you, but you can't leave things like this."

"I know. But what can I do?"

"Call her. Tell her how you feel."

James turned around and hit the ball that he had on the tee. He looked up and watched it climb into the sky and when he lost sight of it in the sun he just turned away. He didn't wait to see it come back down. He walked away and took out his phone. He dialed Mackenzie's number and after four rings it went to voicemail. He was a little upset that she didn't answer, but he didn't blame her after the way he stormed out of her house and didn't respond to any of her calls or text messages. At the tone he simply said, "Hey, it's me. You probably hate me by now, but I was hoping we could talk. Give me a call back. Please."

* * *

Chad brought Mackenzie to the church and helped her set up her classroom. While they worked they caught up on the events of the summer. The conversation turned to James a couple times, but she quickly changed the subject and Chad didn't push it. He wanted to steer clear of that topic himself. If he had any chance of her letting him back into her life he needed to make sure she never found out about the role he played in the break up and right now he wanted to keep her from thinking of him.

When Mackenzie finished everything she had to do for class she decided to call Julie and see if everything was okay. She went to her bag and reached in for her phone but couldn't find it. She began to dig through everything in her bag, but it wasn't there. Chad saw that see was looking for something and asked her if she lost something.

"I was just looking for my phone. I wanted to call and check on Julie but I guess I left it in her car."

"Oh. You can use mine if you want."

"Thanks," she said as she took it from him and dialed her number. Julie didn't answer so she just left a voicemail. "Hey Jul, it's me. I just wanted to check in on you and make sure everything was alright. I think I left my phone in your car so call me at home later. I hope everything is okay. Bye." She hung up and handed the phone back to Chad. "I hate not having my phone. I always feel like I am going to miss something important, you know what I mean?"

"I know exactly what you're talking about, but don't worry, I'm sure she'll call you back in a little bit. Come on, I'll take you home."

She grabbed her things and followed him outside to his car. Just before she got in she stopped. "I just want to thank you for today," she said. "I've had a hard couple of weeks and it's nice to know there are still people who care about me."

"I'll always care about you. You know that."

She leaned into him and gave him a hug before turning to the passenger door and getting into the car.

* * *

Once James and Billy grew tired of hitting golf balls at the driving range they decided to head into town for lunch. On their way to get some pizza they had to drive up the street that the church was on. As they turned onto the block James saw the last thing he ever expected to see. Mackenzie was just standing there halfway up the block.

"Stop the car!" James said quickly as he became overwhelmed with more feelings than he could comprehend at once.

"What?"

"Stop... Now," he said again.

Billy pulled over to the curb and stopped. "What's up?" he asked.

James pointed up the street and Billy saw Mackenzie. "This is perfect," he said. "I'll bring you up there and you can talk to her."

Just as Billy was about to pull back out they saw Chad standing right behind her. Then, before either of them could react she turned, hugged him, and climbed into his car. James felt his heart sink. *That's why she didn't answer her phone*, he thought to himself. *She's with Chad.*

They waited until Chad's car pulled away from the church and then James said, "Get me the hell out of here."

"Are you okay?" Billy asked.

"Not now, Bill," he snapped. "Just take me home."

Twenty-One

It wasn't until the next day that Mackenzie heard from Julie. It was almost noon when the phone rang and when she saw the caller ID she answered right away.

"Oh my God, Julie, is everything okay?"

She responded in a voice that sounded exhausted and as if she had been crying. "It's my father. He went to the hospital last night."

"What happened? Is he going to be alright?"

"We're still here, but they're saying he's going to be fine. He was complaining of chest pains when my mother called me to come home. By the time I got there the pain hadn't gone away so my mom called an ambulance."

"What was it?"

"They have done all sorts of tests and they think it was a very mild heart attack. They said it doesn't look that bad, but they're keeping him here for forty-eight hours for observation and to do a few more tests. If everything checks out they said he will be able to go home."

"Oh, Julie, I should have been there for you. If I knew you know I would have come with you."

"I know, but we didn't know what it was. Don't worry about it. He's going to be fine."

"I can't tell you how glad I am to hear that."

"I know. Oh, by the way, I found your phone. You left it in the cup holder in my car. My mother told me to go home and get some rest, but that is the last thing I can think of doing right now. Would it be okay if I brought it to your house?"

"Of course, but you probably should get some rest."

"I took a couple naps last night in the waiting room. I'll be fine, but I don't want to go home and be alone right now."

"Come over, I'll make us a pot of coffee."

It was about a forty minute ride from the hospital, but because of how tired Julie was it was almost an entire hour before she got there. As soon as Mackenzie opened the door Julie bursted into tears and collapsed into her friends arms. They stood there in the doorway for a good two minutes before Julie was able to pull herself away from Mackenzie and make her way into the living room. They sat down and Mackenzie asked her how she was doing.

"I don't know. I'm just exhausted. Not from being tired. I am. Really tired. But I'm just so mentally exhausted. I can't tell you how hard it was to see him like that. My father has always been the strongest man I've ever known, but now he's just lying there in a hospital bed. When we were first allowed to go in and see him he couldn't even talk without sounding winded. He's gotten better over night, but it was all so scary."

Mackenzie sat there quietly while her friend spoke.

Julie told her about how they were in and out of his room all night. About the tests the doctors did on her father, and how she didn't want to leave his side every time they came in and kicked them out to the waiting room. Eventually, when she started to cry again Mackenzie just held her. She embraced her best friend while she cried until her exhaustion finally caught up with her and she fell asleep on the couch. Mackenzie laid a blanket over her and left her to rest.

Three hours went by before she woke up and walked into Mackenzie's room.

"Hey, how about that cup of coffee you promised me?" she asked.

"Of course, how are you feeling?"

"Better now that I got some rest that wasn't in a hard plastic waiting room chair. Sorry I just crashed like that."

"There is nothing to be sorry about. Come on, let's go to the kitchen."

Mackenzie made a fresh pot of coffee and they sat quietly while they drank. After Julie finished her first cup she remembered she still had Mackenzie's cell phone and she pulled it out of her bag. When Mackenzie looked at it the battery was dead so she plugged it into the charger on the kitchen counter and forgot about it.

They spent another hour together before Julie decided to head back to the hospital. There was no way Mackenzie was going to let her best friend face this alone so she insisted on going with her. When they got there they found out that Julie's father's condition had greatly improved and had been transferred to a private room. They walked in to find him sitting up in the bed and Julie's mother in the chair next to him.

"Daddy, you look great. How are you felling?" Julie asked.

"Oh I'm feeling much better. I just want to get out of this place and go home."

"You heard what the doctor said," her mother responded. "If everything stays the same you can go home tomorrow. Stop rushing it and just relax. You have to recuperate."

"I can recuperate at home. At least there I have ESPN."

"Oh, Daddy, stop it and just get better," Julie said. "Mackenzie came to see how you are feeling."

"Hey Mr. Hart, How are you?"

"I'm fine Mackenzie. Thanks for coming."

"Don't mention it. You guys are like family, I wouldn't think of not being here."

Mackenzie spent the rest of the evening at the hospital and then headed home. Once she got there she grabbed her phone to send Julie a text to let her know she got home okay and to check on her father. After sending the message she saw that she had a message. She dialed into her voicemail and heard the last thing she would have expected.

"Hey, it's me…" As soon as she heard James speak she was instantly overcome with emotion. She was so unbelievably happy to hear his voice, and the sound of it sent chills through her body. Goosebumps rose on her arms and she was immediately reminded of how much she missed him. But then, her feelings of happiness were instantly ripped away from her and replaced with confusion when she heard his next words. "You probably hate me by now…" The words constantly reverberated in her mind. She didn't know what he was talking about... *Why would he think that?* she thought to herself. *If anything I thought he hated me.* The message continued and he said that he wanted to talk. She wanted that more than anything. She didn't know what he wanted to talk about, but she couldn't pass up the chance to apologize for what he heard that night at her house. If she had any chance to clear things up this was it. She couldn't believe that after all this time he finally called and she didn't have her phone. As soon as she hung up from listening to the message she dialed his number.

It rang once...

Please, pick up...

Twice...

Please, come on. Pick up...Pick up...

Three times... Then four...

Damn, it's his voicemail.

"Hi, I just got your message. I would really like to talk, too. Give me a call. Okay, I'll talk to you later. Bye."

Twenty-Two

Four days went by and she still hadn't heard back from him. She wanted nothing more than to call him again…and again…and again, but she knew that wouldn't do anything. She needed to talk to him. She needed to hear his voice again. She wanted nothing more than to have him in her life, but how is that ever going to happen if she can't even get him on the phone so they can talk about things. She just kept wondering why he would call only to ignore her again. She didn't know how it could be so easy for him to just walk away. The only thing that she did know for sure was that she couldn't keep doing this. Her love for him was stronger than anything she ever experienced, but that obviously wasn't enough.

* * *

It had been five days since James saw her with Chad and he couldn't believe that he made a fool out of himself by leaving that message on her phone. And to top it all off, she had the audacity to call him back. Why? What could she possibly have to say to him? *Sorry I led you on and made you think that I loved you, but I got back together with my ex-boyfriend.* Well there was no way that was going to happen. He might have fallen in love with her, but it was obvious that she never felt the same way.

But then why would she have told you she loved you? He heard a voice inside his head say.

"No!" he said out loud. "If she loved me there is no way she would have kept all those things from me. There is no way she would be with Chad now."

But maybe she's not with him. You don't know that for sure, the voice responded.

James had been having this argument with himself ever since he heard that voicemail Mackenzie left on Sunday night. In fact, it's pretty much the only conversation he had with anyone. He wouldn't take any calls from Billy, he wouldn't talk to his father, and Ryan was smart enough to just leave him alone. He had to figure out what he was going to do. He needed to get away from this place. All he knew was he only had one more week to deal with this and then he would be back at school and he could fall back into the routine of real life and forget about this entire summer.

James was sitting on the dock throwing stones into the water when his father came up behind him and sat down. "Hey. How you doing there, James?"

He threw another stone into the water and didn't even look at his father.

"Listen, son, I don't know what has been going on lately, but you know you can always talk to me, right?"

James still didn't respond.

"Well, okay. But I just want you to know, whatever happened to you recently doesn't change the fact that I am glad you came here this summer. I've missed you, and I understand why you haven't wanted to come up here, but it was great to get to know you again." He sat there for a moment and when James still didn't respond he got up and started to walk away.

"Dad, wait!" James called out.

His father turned around and took a seat next to him.

"It's just a bunch of stuff with Mackenzie. I don't know what happened. I don't know how it got to this point."

"Why don't you tell me what happened."

"Well, things were going great," James said. "We were spending every possible minute together and it just felt so right. I never felt that way about anyone before and then, out of nowhere, it all just turned out to be one big lie. An entire summer of deception, and I don't know how any of it happened."

"That's pretty vague, son. Tell me what happened."

James went through the entire story, just like he did with Billy. Again, he didn't have to think about the words. They spilled out of him as if he had been rehearsing the story. In a way he had been. Ever since it happened the scenes of the summer had been playing over and over again in his mind. Every time he hoped he would see something he missed. Some indication that it would end like this, but he never did. As far as he could tell it was all real. The most real thing he had experienced in a long time, but he was obviously wrong.

When he finished the story he took a deep breath to compose himself and his father sat there silently. Finally, Jerry spoke and simply said, "I think you have to call her."

"What good would that do," James yelled defensively. "Weren't you listening? It was all a lie. She never cared, and she's back together with Chad."

"How do you know that? Because you saw them hug? I wouldn't call that concrete evidence. You need to talk to her and figure this all out. I'm not saying that it will lead to you two getting back together, but you need to talk to her. You can't leave things unsaid and unfinished. You need to work it all out so you can move on."

"So you're all insightful now? What would you know about it? And even if I do, what if the threat Chad made was true? What if he can get your contract with North Shore pulled?"

"First of all, I don't care about the damn job. You are my son and I want nothing more in the world than for you to be happy. You do what you have to do for yourself, and if that means I get fired with only a week or two left of the job then so be it. You are more important than any job.

"And secondly, as far as the unfinished business goes, I know it all too well. Did you know that the weekend we came up here before your mother died she and I had a huge fight?" He didn't wait for an answer before he continued. "Of course you didn't, we were always good and keeping that stuff from you boys. Well anyway, even then my business wasn't doing all that well and we were having another fight over which bills would get paid and which ones were going to have to wait until the next paycheck. That's why she hadn't come up with us. The time apart always helped us clear our minds. Next thing I know the state trooper is knocking on our door telling us about the accident.

"I like to think that she was coming up here to work

things out. I like to think that had she made it we would have both apologized to each other. I would have insisted it was entirely my fault, and she would have done the same, and we would have held each other until it didn't matter anymore. But I'll never know now. There was so much that we didn't say to each other. There was so much left for us to do. I have to live with that 'what if' every day. I don't want that for you, son. You have to call her. If nothing else then for closure. You have to call her. Let her tell you what she wants. Let her tell you what everything means. Don't just assume and let it eat at you the rest of your life."

When he was done talking he just stood up, put his hand on his son's shoulder for a moment, and then walked back to the house. James didn't know what to make of what he just heard. He never knew any of that. He never knew that his family had any problems with money and he certainly had no idea that his parents fought over it on a regular basis. He and Ryan always thought that their parents had the best marriage they had ever seen. James had a lot of thinking to do. This new advice from his father made more sense than he ever thought he could get on the topic, but he still didn't know what to do, so he went inside to sleep on it.

* * *

After a long night of restless sleep James still had no idea what he was going to do. He spent half the day sitting at the water, just starring off at nothing while boats floated past. He kept thinking about what his father told him. As much as he hated to admit it, he thought his father was right. He had to talk to her. He had to hear the words from her mouth. If nothing else, he didn't want to live with the regret of not calling her. He didn't want to be haunted by the 'what if'.

He took his phone out of his pocket and starred at it for a long time. He tried to figure out what to say. What if she answered? What if she didn't? All sorts of questions ran through his mind and he felt himself beginning to second guess the idea of calling. Before he let his fears change his mind he dialed her number. The phone rang two and a half times before he heard the most beautiful sound he could imagine...

"Hello? James?"

He froze. All of a sudden a lump grew in the back of his throat and he couldn't speak. He knew he wanted to, but he just couldn't form the words. He couldn't form any words.

"James, are you there?" she asked in a hopeful tone.

The sound of her voice somehow calmed him. She didn't sound as though she hated him. In fact, she almost sounded as if she was glad he called. He took a deep breath and exhaled slowly and then forced out the simplest words he could. "Yeah, I'm here."

Twenty-Three

As glad as James was to be talking to her, he didn't know what to say. He still had so many unanswered questions. He wanted to know how things turned out the way they did. He wanted to know why she didn't feel she could tell him the truth about leaving. He wanted to know so much, but he couldn't find the right words for all the thoughts going through his mind. They spent almost an hour on the phone, but in all that time, they never really got passed small talk. There was more awkward silence than there was conversation and James could tell that she was just as uncomfortable as he was. Finally, Mackenzie suggested that they get together in person.

They decided to meet the next day at the diner for lunch. James got there before Mackenzie so he took a seat at their usual booth. While he sat there waiting for her he couldn't stop his mind from playing out the up-coming afternoon over and over. He saw so many different ways this meeting could go. He saw one version where she told him that she never meant for their relationship to go as far as it did and she was sorry for leading him on. He saw another where she told him that she loved him and didn't want anything to ever come between them again. Then he saw one where she said that she loved him, but since it was so easy for him to walk away from her once she couldn't trust that he wouldn't do it again and she couldn't be with him. He grew more and more nervous as the minutes went by, and then, before he realized it, she walked through the door.

The instant he laid eyes on her his mind became clear. All his visions of the possible ways this day could go wrong were gone and he felt a sense of ease just being in the same room as her. He still had no idea what was about to happen, but he was strangely okay with it. All he could focus on was how beautiful she looked and how much he missed her. As she walked towards the table he felt as if nothing had ever changed between them, and for the first time since he walked out of her house he felt...normal. He felt...relaxed.

When she took the seat across from him they awkwardly said hello to each other and he could feel the tension between them. The uncomfortable feeling of not knowing what was going to happen came rushing back and he found it hard to look her in the eyes, but at the same time, he didn't want to take his eyes off of her. He was happy to be with her and he needed to know what happened between them.

"How have you been?" he asked her.

"I've been alright," she said. "But I've missed you."

This took him by complete surprise. He didn't know how to respond. He looked down at the menu that he had seen so many times just to think about how to respond. He exhaled slowly to calm his nerves and responded. "I've missed you, too."

They finally looked each other in the eyes and he felt like he was someplace else. He felt as if nothing had ever happened and they were still together. Like they belonged together. He started to let out a small smile, but then he stopped himself. He remembered everything *did* happen. He remembered why he was there. He was there for answers, and more importantly, closure.

The waitress came over and took their order. She filled their coffee cups and walked away to punch what they wanted into the computer. James sipped his black coffee while Mackenzie poured the creamers into hers. He could tell she was just as uneasy as he was by the way she continued to stir her coffee long after the creamers were mixed in.

"I'm sorry for the way I barged out of your house that night," he said to break the silence.

"Listen, I know my father can be a jerk, but you have to believe that wasn't all about you. It was about me and his disappointment in me."

"That's not why I left. I mean, yeah, the things he said definitely didn't make me feel very welcome, but I left because everything Chad said was right." Right away James realized what he had just done.

"What do you mean? Everything Chad said? What did he say and why would it make you walk out on me like that?"

"Look, I know you two are seeing each other again and I'm not looking to get in the way of that. He told me..."

"What? We are *not* seeing each other," she interrupted. "What did he say to you? I want to know."

"He told me that there was no way things were going to work out between you and me. I guess he was right, huh? But I know you two are back together. I saw you. You don't have to lie to me."

"James, I don't know what you think you saw, but I assure you, I am not now, nor will I ever be with Chad." She said with a sense of disgust that made James believe her. "Now what else did he say to you? You wouldn't have walked out of my house and ignored me for so long just because he said things weren't going to work between us."

James hesitated for a minute trying to put his thoughts together and think about what he was going to say. "He said… He said that I wasn't right for you. That you were leaving at the end of the summer and that I was nothing more than one last fling for you before you left."

"And you just believed him?" she said with a voice that sounded annoyed. "You believed him and didn't say anything to me? You didn't think to ask me about it."

"Well, no. I mean, not until I heard you with your father. That confirmed everything and I just didn't know what to say to you after that."

Mackenzie suddenly remembered the things that were said during her argument with her father. All she had been focusing on was the stuff he said about James and how much of a disappointment she was for not wanting to go to Princeton. She didn't even think about the fact that he mentioned the mission with the church. She thought about how that must have sounded to James, especially after hearing it from Chad first.

"You were never a fling. I told you I love you and I

meant it. I have never felt the way I feel when I am with you. Now, I know what it feels like to lose you, and I never want to feel like that again. I want to be with you, James." She looked him straight in his eyes as if she were looking straight into his soul. "I love you, James, and I am so sorry that you found out about the mission with the church that way."

"So you are leaving?"

"Yes."

"When?"

"My flight is at nine am tomorrow."

Tomorrow!!! James thought to himself. In an instant, everything that had happened between them, all the reasons he was upset with her, none of it mattered anymore. Suddenly the idea of closure was the last thing on his mind. In the time that they had been sitting together she told him that she still loves him, that she never wants to lose him, and that she is leaving in the morning. He didn't know how this could be happening. All he could think about was how much time he wasted being mad at her. He knew now that nothing would make up for that time, but he had to try. He decided that he had to spend as much time with her as possible until she left. "So what are you doing tonight?" he asked.

"I don't know. Why?"

"Because we don't have a lot of time together before you leave."

"What do you mean, 'we'?"

"Exactly what I said. This summer you have made me feel ways I never thought possible. I've never been happier than when I am with you and I have screwed that up. When you leave, I want us to be on good terms. I want to spend whatever time we have left, together."

"Well, I would like that," she said while she started to blush. "I would like that a lot."

They went back to James' house and she was surprised to see that the pontoon boat was in the water.

"Ryan put the seat covers you made on. They're a perfect fit."

"I'm glad they worked out. I've never made anything like that before."

They decided to take the boat out so James went into the house and packed a cooler. They went out to the middle of the lake and James cut off the motor. They didn't put down the anchor. They just sat there holding each other as the boat drifted in the water. They sat for a long time without saying a word to each other. James just held her while she rested her head in the nook between his chest and shoulder. He couldn't help but notice how perfectly they seemed to fit together. He gently ran his fingers through her hair while he held her close enough to feel her heart beat in unison with his own. Minutes faded into hours and the next thing they knew the sun was beginning to set behind the mountains.

When James started the motor again Mackenzie thought he was going to head back to the house, but instead he pulled up to the old convent boathouse. He stopped in front of the old wooden door and pulled open a panel to the right of it revealing a chain. He used it to pull open the door and slowly pulled the boat inside. It was dark, and if it weren't for the moonlight shining through the cracks in the wood they wouldn't be able to see anything. James took a flashlight from the boat, grabbed the cooler, and led Mackenzie to an old spiral staircase that led to the second floor.

They ended up in a large room that was dark and

looked very old, but it was full of charm and beauty. There was a long wooden table with two equally long benches on either side that must have been where the nuns ate together. Next to that was what appeared to be the living area. There was some old furniture under sheets, a grand piano in the corner, and a fireplace on the far wall. There had to be an inch of dust on everything, but when James started to light candles along the table and the mantel the room seemed to glow. They laid a blanket on the floor below a large skylight in the ceiling and quietly lost themselves in the stars.

James held her as if time didn't exist. He ran his fingers through her hair and wished the night would never end. "Can I ask you a question?" he asked, breaking the silence.

"Anything," she responded without looking away from the sky.

"I don't even know where you're going, what's this mission all about?"

"It's a mission with the church in Haiti. We are going to spend six months there building a new school and helping get it established once it's done. It's an area that has never had their own school and the families can't afford to send their kids anywhere else."

"That sounds like an amazing experience. Why didn't you tell me about it sooner?"

"Because, I didn't know if I was going to go."

"What do you mean? Based on the argument you had with your father it sounded like it was a decision you were pretty set on."

"I was... I mean, I am."

"That doesn't sound very confident."

"Well, I knew more than anything that it was what

I wanted to do. So set on it I didn't even apply to college. I couldn't see going through life with everything I have and not doing anything to help those who struggle over the most basic things. Kids deserve the opportunity to learn. The opportunity to better their lives and the lives of their families. But then... Then I met you."

"Me? What does that mean?"

"Well, everything with you is just so amazing. I love you so much and I don't want to lose you. So, I didn't tell you because I was thinking about not going. I thought I would just look for schools, I don't know, maybe in the Boston area, and we could just be together."

"I wouldn't be able to let that happen."

She spun around to face him and propped herself up on her elbow to bring her face up to his. "Why not?" she asked. "You don't want to be with me?"

"No, that's not it at all." He paused for a moment as if to be sure of the next words that came out of his mouth. "I love you, Mackenzie. I love you because of who you are. Because ever since I met you, if I've learned anything about you, it is that you let people into your heart and in turn, you touch theirs. You have the power to change so many lives. You have the power to change lives the way you have changed mine and it wouldn't be fair to the world for me to keep you from that. As much as I would love for you to stay, to stay with me, I want you to go. I want you to go because there are people out there that *need* you to go."

Mackenzie looked deep into his eyes. "Do you mean that?"

"Every word of it."

"You love me?"

"I love you more than I thought it was ever possible to love another person."

He looked at her with an expression of affection that could never be put into words. He ran his fingers through her hair again and then gently brought it to her cheek. He held her face in his hands, gently caressing her cheekbone with his thumb. The fire behind his stare made her heart skip a beat. He lowered his head to hers while he ran his hand behind her neck and pulled her towards him. He pressed his lips against hers and a chill ran down his spine. He wrapped his arms around her, pulling her into him and kissing her deeper. Everything in the room faded away. Everything else in the world disappeared and it was just them. In that moment nothing else existed. Nothing else mattered.

They made love that night, wishing time would stop and they could live in that moment forever. They spent the night in each other's arms knowing that in the morning Mackenzie was leaving and it would be six months before they could be together again.

The morning sun woke them as it broke the top of the mountain and warmed their faces through the skylight. They slowly packed up their things and made their way back to the boat. When they got back to James' house he walked her to her car. He kissed her again, trying to prolong the moment as much as he could, but ultimately she forced herself to pull away.

"I have to go. My parents are going to be furious that I didn't come home last night and I have to get to the airport."

"I'm going to miss you."

"I'm going to miss you, too," she said. "More than you know. I love you."

"I love you, too."

He stepped back and watched her drive down the street until her car was out of sight.

Twenty-Four

A week had gone by since James last saw Mackenzie, and even though he missed her more than he ever had before, he was in a much better state of mind. He knew that he loved her, and he knew that she loved him. He knew the next six months were going to be tough, especially since Mackenzie didn't have a phone where she was, but they were back together. It was hard for him to understand why he even let such little things get between them in the first place.

Since she left the first thing he did every morning was check his email for a message from her. That was the only form of communication they had with one another. He hadn't received anything by the time he had to leave Roscoe and head back to school. As soon as he got to his dorm the first thing he set up was his computer. He logged into his email account and there it was. The message he had been waiting for.

August 24, 2009

James,

I can't tell you how much I miss you. The flight wasn't that long, but all I could do was think about how hard it is going to be not seeing you for six months. I couldn't wait for them to set up this computer so I could send you this email and tell you that you are all I have thought about since the night in the boat house. That was the most amazing night of my life and I can't wait to be in your arms again.

This place is nothing like home, but it is amazing. All the girls are in one room together, and the guys have their own. I picture it is something like a big dorm room. We only have one computer for everyone, and unfortunately I'm not going to have a lot of time to use it. I promise I will write you as much as I possibly can, and I expect you to do the same. I want to hear about everything that happens at school.

Everyone here is so friendly. They can't wait to have their own school and everyone is ready and willing to help out in any way they can. We have been learning everything we need to know to start building, and now that all the supplies have arrived, we are going to get started tomorrow. I'll write back again soon.

I love you,
Mackenzie

James was glad to finally know that she made it there okay. He knew she probably wasn't going to read it right away, but he didn't waste any time writing her back.

August 24, 2009

Mackenzie,

I miss you, too. It has been hard not hearing from you all week, but I guess I am going to have to get used to it. I am just glad that you have the computer. I couldn't imagine not being able to talk to you at all while you are away.

The night before you left was very special to me, too. I never thought I would connect with someone in my life the way we have connected. You have given me a whole new perspective on life. You have given me faith. Faith in myself, faith in others, and most importantly, you have given me the faith to believe that good things can happen. These are things that I had given up on before I met you, and I want to thank you for that.

Anyway, I am back at school now and that should help me cope with not being with you. I have the same roommate as last year, Rob, I don't think I told you too much about him. We don't have all that much in common, but he is a great guy that always knows how to cheer people up. He is the type of person that you can't avoid having fun with, and he's always the life of the party. I told him all about the amazing summer we had together and he assured me that he will keep me busy so our time apart goes by as quickly as possible.

You be careful doing all that work. Construction is not an easy job, but I know you will do great and make something amazing for those kids. They are lucky to have you.

I can't wait to see you again.

I love you,
James

Twenty-Five

It had been more than two weeks since James got that first email from Mackenzie. During that time he sent one more message to her, about a week after the first. He told her he was just writing to tell her about his class schedule, but the truth was that he just missed her, and even if she didn't get it right away it made him feel better to write to her. Once classes started, James noticed that time seemed to go by a little quicker than it did during that first week. The first thing he still did every morning was check his email for a new message from her. It had sort of become a ritual for him. After that he would get ready for the day and head out. He spent the day going from one class to another and hanging out with Rob and some of his other friends in the student center when he had a break.

Rob was a DJ with the school radio station and seemed to know everyone on campus. No matter what time of day it was, Rob always seemed to be in the student center, which worked out well for James because he always had someone to hang out with. James had just gotten out of his Contemporary Metaphysics class and headed to the student center to get a cup of coffee. Rob was there with some of the guys from the station, so James took a seat at their table.

"Hey, Jim, what's going on?"

"Not much. What's going on with you guys?"

"Just got out of class. What are you doing tonight? The radio station is having a party, kind of a 'back to school' thing. You should come with."

"I don't know, man."

"Come on, what else do you have to do?"

"Nothing really."

"So you should come. It's not going to be anything too crazy, just a bunch of us getting together, talking about how awesome our summers were."

"Alright, fine. I'll stop by for a while." James was surprised at how much Rob reminded him of Billy by the way he could talk him into doing things.

Later that night when James got to the party it looked more like a frat house than a dorm. There were people all over the place, loud music coming from a DJ table, and a keg in the corner. It took a couple minutes to maneuver through all the people. When James finally found Rob he was sitting on a couch in the back of the room with a group of people.

"Hey, there he is," Rob yelled over the music. "Slide over. Make some room for my roommate."

Everyone quickly listened, except for the girl next to him that he had his arm around.

"I thought you said this was going to be a small get together. I believe your exact words were, 'nothing crazy'. This is nuts. I can't believe all these people even fit in here."

"Yeah, what can I say, I guess word got out," he responded with a laugh that insinuated anything smaller wouldn't be any fun.

"I'd say so."

"Anyway, you know Dave from the station. This is Tara," he pointed to the girl who was hanging on Dave. "This is Lindsey, she's a new freshman here," he said introducing the girl he had his arm around, "and this is Sara, her roommate," nodding towards the girl sitting on the other side of him on the couch.

After about an hour of hanging out Rob and Lindsey had left together, Dave and Tara were making out in the corner, and James found himself sitting on the couch alone with Sara. They talked about where they were from, their classes, and how much of a change Boston was from where Sara had grown up. It started to get late, and with Lindsey still not back Sara asked James if he would mind walking her back to her room.

They walked quietly across campus until they got to Sara's dorm building, which happened to be the same building James lived in. It was a large coed building that separated males and females by floor.

"Well, I found our roommates," Sara said with a giggle when they got to her room.

"What do you mean?" James asked.

"She hung a scarf on the door. She said that was going to be the sign if we weren't alone in the room. I told her it was corny, but I guess it does the trick."

"I guess they really hit it off."

"Yeah, but now I have no place to go."

"Hey, just come upstairs to my room."

"Are you sure?"

"It's fine. What am I supposed to do, leave you sitting in the hall? Besides, it's not like my roommate will mind."

They laughed and made their way up to James' room. When they got there he told her to make herself comfortable and got her a drink. They sat up for hours talking. They talked about their favorite music, movies, and books. It turned out they had a lot in common and it seemed like they were never going to run out of things to talk about. Eventually, the conversation turned to relationships.

"So, are you seeing anyone, James?" she asked.

"Actually I am."

"Oh, does she go to school here?"

"No, she doesn't."

Sara could tell by the tone in his voice that he missed her.

"Long distance relationship, huh? They can be hard. I should know. My boyfriend, Todd, is at the University of Alabama. I haven't seen him since I left for school. What's your girlfriend's name? Where does she go to school?"

"Her name is Mackenzie, but she's not at school. She is on a church mission in Haiti. They're building a school there."

"Haiti. Wow. That is so amazing."

"Yeah, but it is tough being so far apart. She doesn't even have a phone. All we can do is email back and forth."

"Well, it's better than nothing. My boyfriend is right here in the country and I still don't hear from him as often as I would like. I know I just got here, but sometimes I don't know if it's going to work out."

They talked about their relationships for the rest of the night until they eventually fell asleep. When James woke up Sara was still sleeping and Rob still wasn't back. He showered and then sat down at his computer. Finally, there was another email from Mackenzie.

September 12, 2009

James,

Sorry it has been so long since I last wrote you, there just isn't a lot of time to get online and we have a very touchy electrical system here because it is hurricane season. The power is constantly going down. Besides that, I can't even tell you how incredible it is to be here and be a part of this mission. I am really starting to get the hang of this construction thing, but that is not what is so great. It's not even the fact that we are building a school. It's getting to know the people here. They are all such beautiful people. There is this one little girl who I am absolutely in love with. She is so cute. Her name is Astryd and she is seven years old. She is the brightest little girl I have ever met. I can't even tell you how excited she is to be able to finally go to school. Until now, it has only been a dream to her and her friends.

Astryd is such a huge part of my day. She follows me around doing anything she can to help. She carries supplies, brings water to the other workers, and just tries her best to be a part of the whole process. When we get a

*break from work I play with her and help her
learn to read. Her favorite game is to set up
some dolls and pretend she is a teacher. It is
so adorable.*

*It is amazing how strong these people are,
too. Things we grew up taking for granted
they've never even had. They have experienced
things you and I could never imagine,
however, they are constantly happy. It is an
appreciation of life I have never seen before.*

*I wish you were here to experience all of
this with me. I miss you so much.*

Love,
Mackenzie

Just as he was writing her back Rob came fumbling
through the door. He saw James sitting at his desk, his
hair still wet and wearing a pair of sweatpants and an
undershirt. "Oh, dude. You brought her back to the
room? That a boy."

"It's not like that, Rob. She had no place to go since
you were in her room. We just hung out."

"Okay, bud, whatever you want to tell yourself."

"Really."

With all the conversation Sara woke up. "Just getting
home? I guess you had a good night," she said.

"Just about as good as yours," Rob responded.

"Stop it, James was a perfect gentleman." She
grabbed her things to head back downstairs. "I had a
nice time. I hope we can hang out again soon."

Twenty-Six

As the semester went on James and Mackenzie finally fell into a routine and emailed back and forth at least once a week. Once James knew when to expect her messages, although he still missed her, he felt a little closer to her again. They talked about everything. They talked about what was happening at school and how his classes were going. They talked about her mission and how much of a difference her team was making for the people they were helping. No matter how much he missed her, he was proud of her for everything she was doing, and he was glad she was having the experience of a lifetime. He knew that she was doing everything she could to help change the world and that was a big part of why he loved her.

As hard as it was not being with her, his day to day life at school had gotten easier as time went on. He didn't look at it as he got used to not seeing her, because he knew he could never get used to something like that, he looked at it like he had good friends that understood how hard a long-distance relationship was. Especially

Sara, who he had been seeing a lot of ever since the night of the party, now that Rob and her roommate Lindsey were dating. If anyone knew what it was like to be away from the person you loved it was her. Granted her boyfriend was in the same country as her, and they were able to talk on the phone just about whenever they wanted, but she was the closest person to understanding what it was like for him, and as a result they became close friends.

As it turned out they had a lot in common. Besides both being in a long-distance relationship, they liked the same music, the same books, and on a deeper level, they had both lost a parent. Sara lost her father at a very young age. They only talked about it once. Mostly because she didn't really know a lot about what had happened. He was a firefighter and it happened on the job. That was the most detail she ever got about it. All she could remember of the night he died was being woken up in the middle of the night by the sound of the doorbell and hearing her mother crying for hours. As she got older, anytime she asked about it, all everyone did was assure her that her father died a hero.

They both also took their classes very seriously, so they ended up talking about school a lot. The only issue with that was they had very different majors and constantly argued over whose was more important. James was a philosophy major and believed that reason and logic were the only way to understand everything. Sara, on the other hand, was a psychology major and was convinced that the most important thing was to understand the way the human mind works. After finals one night Rob, Lindsey, Sara, and James got together to have some dinner and unwind a little. When Rob and Lindsey walked into the room Sara was already there and she and James were in the middle of one of their infamous debates.

"You can't understand anything until you answer the most fundamental questions of life and existence," James said. "We need to look at everything, and only through the application of logic and reason will we find the truth."

Sara countered his argument with the same response she always did. "That is a reasonable argument, but it has one inherent flaw that you constantly overlook."

"And what is that?" James asked, knowing exactly what she was going to say.

"You're overlooking the fact that understanding existence in the world means absolutely nothing if we can't understand the people that live in it. We need to understand everything we can about the human mind and the way it works. That's where we will find answers."

"But those are miniscule answers in comparison to philosophy. If we could understand existence as a whole then we can understand everything that exists...including the human mind."

"Philosophy has no answers. It focuses on unanswerable questions and applies logic to theories. There is nothing definitive there. Psychology is science. It is built on fact, not your concept of *truth*."

"Over and over you two have the same argument and it's driving me crazy," Rob interrupted. "When are you two just going to hook up?"

"Rob, stop," Lindsey said with a laugh.

"No, I'm serious. It really is too bad that you two

are already in relationships with other people because you are absolutely perfect for each other."

"That's not true," Sara said with her head down, trying to hide the fact that she was blushing.

"Yes it is and you know it. You two bicker like you're already married. That's the makings of a perfect union right there."

"You don't know what you're talking about," James said defensively and glared at Rob.

"Now, now, take it easy. It was just a joke."

In hopes to end the conversation Lindsey cut in and said, "Why don't we just go eat?"

"I think that is a good idea," Sara agreed.

They went to a local restaurant and ate while they talked about their exams and how happy they were that the semester was almost over. Then they talked about their plans for winter break. Sara was going home and was going to see her boyfriend. She couldn't wait to see him. It was just about the only thing she had talked about all week. James was going back to the lake, and unlike the summer, he couldn't wait to see his family. Then Rob announced his plans. Lindsey had invited him to go home with her and spend the holidays with her family, and to James' surprise, he was going. James never knew Rob to be so serious about a girl. Rob always seemed to be seeing someone, sometimes even more than one someone, but he never stayed with the same girl longer than a couple of weeks, so when he started seeing Lindsey, James didn't expect much different. Now, it was obvious he had really fallen for her.

* * *

After dinner the girls went back to their room and Rob

and James went back to theirs. The next day was the last official day of school before the break and they both had to finish packing. James knew Lindsey was more than one of Rob's usual flings, the fact that they were together all semester was proof enough of that, but he couldn't believe that he was going home with her. He had to get more details.

"So, meeting the parents, huh?"

"Yeah, man. I'm pretty nervous. I keep thinking I'm going to screw up somehow. You know, do or say something completely stupid and end up getting kicked out of the house or something."

"Trust me, I know the feeling. How come you didn't tell me about this?"

"I wasn't too sure about it myself. Lindsey mentioned it a few weeks ago but we didn't really talk about it much after that. We didn't make any definite plans until earlier this week."

"So, this thing must be more real than I thought."

"It's something about her. She got under my skin and I just can't shake her."

"Yeah, and you love every minute of it."

"Yeah, man, I kinda do. But enough about me, what's the deal with you and Sara? I mean really?"

"There is no deal. We're just friends."

"Listen, I know I bust your balls a lot about her, but I really don't know how you do it. You have this beautiful girl that you spend almost all your time with, and have everything in common with, and you are going to tell me that you are just friends. How is that possible?"

"I love my girlfriend. You know that."

"Yeah, I do. But don't you just miss being with someone? Don't you miss having someone close?"

"I do. But I don't just miss having *someone*. I miss having Mackenzie. I like Sara, a lot, and you're right, we do have a lot in common and she is a great person. Maybe if things were different there could have been more to it, but I'm with Mackenzie. I love her and I couldn't imagine being with anyone else."

"Yeah, I hear ya. You're lucky that you found that person. I was just sayin."

"Yeah, yeah."

They both went to sleep after that. Rob had to wake up early to drive to Lindsey's and James had a bus to catch.

Twenty-Seven

Winter break ended and James went back to school. He got back the day before classes started and was surprised to find that Rob wasn't there yet. They had been rooming together since they started college and after every break Rob was always the first one back. He was always completely unpacked and settled by the time James got there, almost as if he had never left at all, but this time the room was empty. James figured he would take that as a sign that things went well between him and Lindsey over the break and he started unpacking his bags. He was just about finished when he heard the door open behind him.

"It's about time you got here," James yelled without looking, assuming it was Rob coming in behind him.

"Welcome back to you, too," he heard Sara respond.

"Hey. It's good to see you," he answered in surprise. "Sorry about that, I thought you were Rob."

"Don't worry about it. How was your break?"

James went on and on for a while about everything that happened at home. He told Sara about how well his father's business had picked up since he left for school, and how happy both he and his brother seemed. Then he asked if there was any word from Rob and Lindsey.

"I spoke to Lindsey a couple times over the break. She said that her family loved Rob and everything went great. They will be back tomorrow morning."

"That's great. I'm glad things are working out for them. How about you? How was your break? It had to be great to see your boyfriend again after so long."

Sara's expression went blank for a moment and then she looked down at the floor like she was trying to fight off tears.

"Sara, what is it? Is everything okay?"

She just stood there and started to cry. James brought her to a chair and sat her down.

"Sara, tell me what happened."

"Everything was perfect," she said. "When I first got home I couldn't wait to see him so I went straight to his house. For the first few days it was like nothing had ever changed. We were inseparable. We couldn't keep our hands off each other. It was just like it used to be. We spent two days together before I finally went home to see my family. Then, after about a week he started acting weird. One night we were watching a movie and he kept getting up and walking away. He would go into the kitchen or the bathroom and then come right back only a minute or so later. That's not like him, he hates missing parts of a movie. I told myself it was no big deal and not to look too into it so I played it off like I didn't even notice.

"Later that night when he was driving me home he

stopped at a gas station and when he was inside paying his cell phone vibrated and fell off the visor. I only intended to pick it up and put it back for him. I had no intention of looking at it but there was a text message on the screen. I didn't know what to make of it when I read it. **Hurry up and drop off that pain in the ass girlfriend of yours...I have a surprise for you.** Before I could even try to make sense of it another text came through. It was a picture of Vicki, a girl we went to high school with, wearing the skankiest lingerie I have ever seen. I can't even tell you what that did to me, James. I went through the entire thread between the two of them and it went back for months. He had been seeing her the entire time I was gone, who knows, maybe even longer. It felt like my heart was being ripped out of my chest.

"When he got back in the car I told him to drive me home. It took everything not to cry in front of him. I wasn't going to give him that satisfaction. I couldn't. Anyway, when we got to my house I told him I was done with him and I never wanted to see him again. He tried to play it off like he didn't know why I was upset. I threw his phone at him and told him he could ask his *pain in the ass girlfriend* and it would probably make perfect sense.

"I avoided him for the rest of the next week, not that he tried all that hard to get through to me. He called a couple times, sent me a pathetic apology in a text and even called my parents' house. I didn't respond to any of it and within a few days his attempts stopped completely. He didn't care. He didn't love me. After Christmas I just packed up and came back to school. I can't tell you how miserable and lonely it was being the only person on campus, but I couldn't stand being anywhere near him. I had to get away from all of it."

James listened as Sara talked and he felt so bad for her. He knew how much she loved her boyfriend and couldn't imagine what she had to be going through. He could tell that she was really hurting and was pretty sure she didn't want to be alone anymore. He offered to let her stay in his room for the night. He was pretty sure Rob wouldn't mind if she used his bed, and he figured that she had probably been alone on campus long enough.

They spent most of the night just talking. Well, she talked, James pretty much just listened and was there for her while she vented. At times she cried, other times she yelled, and at one point she even slammed her fist into Rob's desk...which just ended up causing more crying. James didn't really know what to say or do, but he knew she needed to get it all out. She talked and cried until she eventually fell asleep. James put a blanket over her, shut off the light, and went to sleep himself.

* * *

The next morning James woke up early. Rob still wasn't back yet and Sara was still sleeping. He went to his desk and set up his laptop. As soon as it booted up he logged into his email and found a new message from Mackenzie. He opened it right away.

January 3, 2010

James,

I have great news...We finally have a definite date for when we are coming home!!! My time here has been nothing short of amazing, but I can't wait to see you. That is why I set it up so I will be flying into Boston. I will be landing at Logan International at one o'clock in the afternoon next Friday, the fifteenth. That is less than two weeks away! I was hoping we could spend the weekend together before I go home to see my family, I hope that is okay with you.

I love you,
Mackenzie

James couldn't believe what he had just read. It may have been a short email, but it was definitely the best one he had gotten from Mackenzie in the entire time she had been gone. He didn't waste any time and wrote her back right away.

January 4, 2010

Mackenzie,

You hope that is okay with me? Is that a joke? I wouldn't have it any other way. That is the best news I have gotten in a long time. I can't wait to see you again. Words don't exist for how much I have missed you. I will be there waiting when you get off the plane.

Love,
James

Sara woke up just as James finished writing back to Mackenzie and for her sake he immediately tried to hide his excitement. His attempts were pointless. No matter how hard he tried he couldn't stop smiling.

"What are you so happy about?" she asked, smiling back at him.

"It's nothing. How are you feeling?"

"I'm a little better now. Thanks for letting me vent, I'm sure that's not how you wanted to spend your night. I think I just really needed someone to talk to."

"That's what friends are for," he said as he walked over to her and gave her a small kiss on the top of her head.

"So really, what are you so happy about this morning?" she asked again.

He didn't want to answer. She had just spent the entire night telling him how her boyfriend ripped her heart out and he was sure the last thing she wanted to hear was good news about his girlfriend, but he couldn't contain himself.

"I got an email from Mackenzie. She's coming home. She'll be here the end of next week."

"Oh my god! That is great news. Why didn't you tell me that right away?"

"I didn't think that was the type of thing you would want to hear right now."

"That is absolutely the type of thing I would want to hear right now. Just because my *EX*-boyfriend is a jackass, that doesn't mean I'm incapable of being happy for you. You are my best friend and that is great news. When do I get to meet her?"

"Well she's coming here. To Boston. I'm picking her up from the airport next Friday and we are spending the weekend together before she goes back to New York.

"That's great. I'm happy for you and I can't wait to meet her."

After that Sara headed back to her room to get ready for the first day of classes for the new semester.

Twenty-Eight

As the week went on James only got more excited about his upcoming reunion with Mackenzie. He couldn't stop thinking about what it would be like to be with her again. To hold her again. To kiss her again. It was a good thing it was only the first week of the semester because he couldn't concentrate on his classes at all. All he could do was run the days of their soon to be weekend together over and over in his head. What it would be like to watch her appear from the crowd in the airport. What it would be like trying to keep his hands off her on the way back to campus. What it would be like once he got her back to the dorm.

He had to keep pushing the thoughts out of his mind. He had to find a way to control himself, to control his thoughts, and focus on his schedule until she got there. He came up with a plan. A plan he could only hope would work. He was going to focus on school during the day, but once he got out of class, he was going to plan out every minute of every day he had with Mackenzie. There was so much he wanted to do with her, but he only had one weekend. He wanted to show her the city. He wanted her to see the campus. He wanted her to meet his friends. But most of all, he just wanted to be with her. As much as he wanted to do everything with her, he wanted to be selfish and keep her all to himself. He wanted to bring her to his room and not let her out of his sight again.

On the Saturday before she got there she sent him an email.

January 9, 2010

Six more days until I get to see you.

I love you,
Mackenzie

It was short. It was simple. But he loved it.

The next two days went by without a word from her, but that didn't stop him from writing. He sent short, simple messages, just as she did on Saturday. He wasn't sure when she would see them, but it still made him feel better sending them.

* * *

James wanted to make sure things were perfect for Mackenzie when she got there. He wanted to get her whatever supplies she might need for the weekend. He also planned on decking out the room to make it more inviting to her. He went online to get ideas on how to decorate a dorm room and make it look more romantic. He found a picture of a room that looked similar to his, not that many dorm rooms were too different, that had the ceiling lined with small Christmas lights and candles all over. It was perfect. It was exactly the type of thing he was looking for. Some soft lighting, a comfortable feel, but not too overdone. He went online to find a place where he could get everything he needed but what he found was overwhelming. The Christmas lights were easy to find, but the candles, that was a whole other story. He knew they came in different shapes and sizes. He knew they came in different scents, obviously, but what he couldn't wrap his mind around was just how many different scents there actually were. There were more options than he knew existed. There were scents that he couldn't even pronounce. He even found one website that talked about mixing several scents together to create the *perfect mood* like there was some kind of science behind it. He was more confused than ever and realized he had no idea what he was doing.

It was Tuesday when Sara promised James she would go shopping with him. He had classes that day from noon until four forty-five, and when his last class let out, he rushed back to his room to get ready. It was just about five o'clock when his phone rang. He looked at it and saw it was Sara calling. He answered hurriedly as he rushed around the room.

"Hey, I'll be ready to go in fifteen minutes. I woke up late this morning and I want to jump in the shower real quick."

"James," she said with an obvious shake in her voice, "turn on the TV."

"Why? What is it?" He didn't know what it was, but he could hear the urgency in her voice.

"Just turn it on, James. Any channel."

James reached for the remote and did as she said.

"If you're just joining us we are here with breaking news. Haiti has just experienced the largest earthquake in the region's history measuring a 7.0...."

The phone dropped to the floor from James' hand and the voice of the news anchor faded in and out. He couldn't focus. He tried his best but only caught random words of the broadcast.

"Thousands dead…"

"Screams…"

"Trapped victims…"

James shook himself out of the trance he was in and flipped from channel to channel. He couldn't stop watching the news. When one program ended he switched to another, but he just kept hearing the same information over and over and over. Hours went by and his body still shook. He felt like his lungs stopped breathing and his heart stopped beating. He felt like he was outside his body watching himself watch the news. Watching himself worry about Mackenzie. He felt helpless. He didn't know what to do.

Then it hit him. He could call the church. Maybe they would know something. He found his phone on the floor, still lying where it landed when he first dropped it hours earlier, and scrolled through his contact list. He found the number that Mackenzie had stored in there in case he ever had to call her at the classroom and hit the call button. It rang and rang, and he prayed and prayed that someone would answer.

NOTHING!

"Damn it!" he shouted and he dialed the number again.

More rings.

More prayers.

Same result.

He wasn't giving up. He couldn't give up. He called the number one more time. One ring...two rings...

"Hello?" someone said with a cracking voice that was obviously crying.

"Oh my God, hello... Thank God someone answered. My name is James Collins. I'm calling because of what's going on in Haiti..."

"James? Mackenzie's friend, right? This is Father O'Reilly. It's horrible. Just horrible."

"Father O'Reilly? What are you doing there? I thought you were there with the group?"

"I was. I... I..." He took a deep breath to stabilize the overflow of emotions that came out of his mouth every time he attempted to speak. "I came home two days ago in order to prepare for their homecoming."

"Have you heard anything? Are they okay? Is Mackenzie okay?"

"I don't know, James. I haven't heard a thing. I've tried to reach anyone I can over there but nothing is working. I wish I had more information for you. I am flying back out there first thing tomorrow. As soon as we know something I will be sure you are contacted."

With that James hung up and prayed for a miracle.

* * *

The next few days went by with a blur. James didn't go to any of his classes. He couldn't. He didn't leave his room for food. He hardly even slept except when he fell asleep against his will. He couldn't risk missing any update on Mackenzie's whereabouts. All he did was watch the news and sit by the phone. Hoping, praying that it would ring and somebody would have some kind of information. Any information. He repeatedly checked his email, knowing there wouldn't be one, but he had to look. He had been watching the news for so long he wasn't even listening to the reporters anymore. He found himself starring at the pictures in the background, trying to see if he could find any trace of her. He knew it was ridiculous, but he hoped to see her in the background digging through the rubble, helping with the rescue efforts.

Early Friday morning he was woken up by the ringing of the phone that was clenched in his hand. He didn't even remember falling asleep but he was instantly pulled into reality and he answered it. "Hello," he said eagerly.

There was a momentary silence on the other end of the line, and then he heard the sound of someone exhale hard as if they were holding their breath.

"Hello?" he said again. "Is someone there?"

"Hello James. It's Martha, Mackenzie's mother." She became silent again, except for the sound of her crying. "Father O'Reilly told me to call you once we knew anything. I had to go through her room to find your number, but we got news a couple hours ago."

James heard her words, but what he was focused on was the sound of her crying. He started to shake again. He started to cry. He knew what she was about to say but he cut her off anyway. "What is it? Did they find her? Is she okay?"

Now Martha was hysterical. James fell apart at the sound of her sobs.

"She didn't make it. They found her last night."

James' world caved in around him with her words. The room started to spin and he fell to the ground. He clenched his eyes shut, grabbed his face and yelled into his palms. He screamed. He cried uncontrollably. His body trembled as he tried to control his breathing and brought the phone back to his ear. "It can't be true," he said. "She was supposed to come home today. It can't be true."

Martha continued to tell him everything she knew. "She was under debris from a building that collapsed. They said when they found her she had her arms wrapped around a little girl. They said that it looked like she was trying to protect her, but there was no way they would have been able to get out."

"I can't believe it. How could this be happening?"

"I don't know, James. It's not fair. She didn't deserve this. No one deserves this. I have to go, but I had to call you myself. I know how much she loved you and I wanted you to hear it from me. I'll be in touch with you soon."

James got off the phone and he still felt like he couldn't breathe. He couldn't wrap his mind around everything he just heard. He loved Mackenzie more than he ever thought it was possible to love someone and now he was never going to see her again. He couldn't believe this was how it ended.

She was gone!

Twenty-Nine

Two and a half years later

The large room was filled with the chattering sound of people as they mingled about. Some sat in the chairs that were spread out around the floor, some were at a refreshment table talking over a cup of coffee and cookies, and others just lingered around aimlessly by themselves. James stood off to the side in the front of the room with Father O'Reilly watching as the small crowd slowly settled in. He was so tense that he could feel his nerves rising up into his throat to the point that it felt like there was something physically cutting off his breathing. This was the very moment he had been focusing on since Mackenzie died. The first day of the rest of his life. But now that it was staring him in the face, he didn't know if he could go through with it.

"Are you ready?" Father O'Reilly asked as he turned to James and put his hand on his shoulder.

"It's a lot more people than I thought it would be."

"Everything will be just fine, you'll see. Just believe in yourself."

Father O'Reilly turned and started to walk towards the center of the room where a lectern stood in front of the chairs. When he reached a point that was about half-way there he stopped, turned his head back to James, and gave him one last nod to make sure he was ready. James hesitated, but he nodded back knowing that he was as ready as he would ever be.

When Father O'Reilly reached the lectern he loudly knocked on the wooden top and addressed the crowd. "Okay everyone, if you could please find a seat we are about to get started."

The numerous conversations began to fade as everyone shuffled to a seat and turned their attention to the front of the room.

"Good evening everybody. I see a lot of familiar faces tonight, but I also see some new ones and that is great. For those of you that haven't been here before my name is Father O'Reilly. Welcome.

"Now, things are going to be a little different to-night. I would like to introduce a young man that is very special to me. Some of you may know him as he has been to these meetings before, but tonight he is here in a different context. Tonight he is going to be taking on the role of facilitator, so without any further introduc-tion, James please come on up."

James slowly walked to the front of the room and took his place in front of the lectern. "Hello, my name is James. James Collins. You have to forgive me, I'm a little nervous. Thank you all for coming tonight. Before we talk about anything tonight I think it is only fair that I tell you a little bit about myself. Like many of you I have lost someone that was very important to me.

"I lost my mother about five years ago in a horrible

car accident. After she passed away I had no idea how to cope. I had never lost anyone like that before. Sure I had other relatives pass away, but they all lived full lives and grew old. We had time to prepare for their deaths. But my mother was so young. It wasn't her time. It was a tragedy that no one was ready for. I shut out the pain. I avoided the places that reminded me of her. I thought that would be enough. I thought I could go on with my life and just not think about it. That was until it was all shoved right back in my face.

"One summer I had no choice but to stay with my family at our lake house. The house that stood only about a half mile away from where my mother died. I didn't want to be there. Looking back at it now I can see that the pain I felt from the memory of my mother's death had manifested itself as anger. I resented that place. Those roads. The world.

"Then I met someone. Another person that became very special to me. Mackenzie. She helped me to realize that I didn't have to be angry. She taught me that I didn't need to block everything out. Quite the opposite actually. I had to remember. Not how she died, but how she lived. All the good times I had with her. All the things she shared with me that made me who I was. That was the only way to really move forward. Mackenzie taught me how to be me again. She taught me how to be happy, and I will always love her for that.

"When that summer ended I went back to school and Mackenzie went off to save the world. She dedicated her life to helping others. People that really needed it. She was in Haiti when the earthquake hit."

James bowed his head and pinched the bridge of his

nose in an attempt to hold back tears. After a brief moment he wiped under his eyes and looked back up at the group. "When I got the news that she didn't make it I felt the weight of the world fall on me. I didn't know how I would be able to live without her. I'm not going to lie and say I wasn't angry. I was. I was very angry. How could this happen to someone that put the lives of so many others before their own. It wasn't fair. But then again, death is never really fair, is it?

"Eventually I remembered everything I learned from her. I thought about what she would say if she were still with me. She would have told me that you can't dwell on what you lost, but remember what you had. Times of loss are certainly hard times, but they are also defining moments of one's life. In the most extreme sense it is like a crossroads. Of course, you don't have to pick any one direction right away, there is a proper grieving process that must take place, but eventually a choice has to be made. You can choose a path of anger, resentment, and constant pain, or you can remember the times you had with the one you lost. You can learn from all the experiences, both the good and the bad, and you can allow them to help you become the person you are supposed to be.

"After that everything had changed. I went back to school after the funeral and changed my major to psychology with a concentration in counseling and now I am half way through my master's program. That is why Father O'Reilly has agreed to let me help facilitate these meetings. Through me, and through all of you, our loved ones can live on in our memories. I want to help people the way Mackenzie helped me. If I do that, in a way, her spirit will live on forever."

www.ingramcontent.com/pod-product-compliance
Lightning Source LLC
Chambersburg PA
CBHW031308120626
46554CB00001BA/338